BABY DRAMA

SANDI LYNN

SANDI LYNN ROMANCE, LLC

BABY DRAMA

New York Times, USA Today & Wall Street Journal Bestselling Author
Sandi Lynn

Baby Drama

Copyright © 2021 Sandi Lynn Romance, LLC

❀ Created with Vellum

MISSION STATEMENT

Sandi Lynn Romance

*Providing readers with romance novels that will whisk them away
to another world and from the daily grind of life – one book at a time.*

INTRODUCTION

Jenna

There are two things you need to know about me: I'm very independent and I'm a genius. Literally, I'm a genius. At least that's what my IQ score says. But even being a genius, mistakes are bound to happen. I am human, after all. It all started one night when a sexy billionaire bought me a drink and I accidentally tossed it all over his five-thousand-dollar suit. He tried to blame me, but in actuality, it was his fault because of his lack of respect for my personal boundaries. I offered to pay for the dry cleaning and gave him my number to let me know how much it cost. He did, and we ended up spending the night together. Long story short, the condom broke, I forgot to take my pill two days in a row and we mistakenly created a baby. I never planned on telling him about the baby until I lost my job, and my landlord turned the apartments I lived in into condos. He told me he couldn't be a father, and I was okay with that. I didn't need a man complicating my life. I was all set to embark on my journey as a single parent until...

Lucas

The only thing I did was notice a beautiful woman and buy her a drink. A drink she carelessly spilled all over me and then had the nerve to say it was my fault. I forgave her because I wanted her. At least for one night. Maybe I should have just forgotten about her and thrown her number away. But I didn't, and a mishap occurred during our one-night stand that resulted in a baby. I wasn't father material, or maybe I was, but just didn't want to be. The last thing I needed in my life was baby drama. I liked my bachelor life the way it was, and Jenna was cool with that. She made it clear she didn't want me involved. I was all set to continue on with my life as if nothing happened until...

CHAPTER 1

*J*enna

We slipped in the club among the crowd and made a beeline for the bar. It was opening night for JAMS, a brand-new club we were exclusively invited to, thanks to Bri's boyfriend Carson, who designed the place.

"Carson did a really good job with the place. Don't you think?" Bri shouted over the loud music that had the place shaking.

"Sure." A fake smile fell upon my lips.

I couldn't stand Carson, and Bri knew it. In fact, Carson knew it too. And he couldn't stand me because he knew he couldn't pull one over on me. They'd only been dating about six months and he'd already managed to get her to move in with him. Leaving me alone in the apartment we shared and leaving me with the entire rent and utilities. If he was a decent guy, I would be happy for her, but he wasn't. We tolerated each other for Bri's sake. He was a control freak and he liked to control her. She was weak and vulnerable, and he knew it the moment he met her. What he didn't bargain for was me, the best friend, who was strong and who didn't and wouldn't put up with his bullshit.

1

"What can I get you?" the masculine bartender asked as he leaned over the counter.

"Scotch. One ice cube only." I pointed at him.

"Got it." He grinned.

"And for you?" he asked Bri.

"She'll have a cosmopolitan. Light on the liquor," Carson interrupted.

"She can order her own drink," I scowled at him.

"She could. But I'm here and ordered it for her." His eye narrowed at me.

Douchebag.

"It's fine, Jenna. He knows exactly what I like."

"That's right, baby." He smiled as he hooked his arm around her.

Rolling my eyes, the bartender set my drink down in front of me. Picking it up, I didn't hesitate to throw more than half of it down the back of my throat. As I scanned the club, the dance floor was no longer visible. Every single space of it was occupied with people dancing and having a great time.

"Let's go dance!" Bri smiled as she grabbed my hand.

"Hold on." I downed the rest of my scotch and set my glass on the bar.

Carson followed us to the dance floor. *Of course he did.* Bri wasn't allowed to be out of his sight for two seconds. Magically, space opened up for us as a group of people left the floor and headed to their tables. We moved to the beat of the music, our hands in the air as we jumped up and down, making us feel alive and forgetting our daily problems. I was so lost in the music, I didn't even notice the guy behind me was sexually moving his hips to grind up against me. I'd finally noticed when I felt something hard press against my ass. Turning around, I glared at him.

"You're in my space," I shouted.

"I happen to like your space, baby."

"Is that so?" I asked as I continued dancing.

"Yeah. How about we get out of here so I can invade more of your space?"

2

I placed my hands on his shoulders, bit down on my bottom lip in a seductive way and batted my pretty blue eyes at him. As I leaned in to whisper something in his ear, I lifted my knee and pulverized his balls.

"WTF!" He fell to his knees as he held on tightly to his balls.

"Don't you ever, and I mean ever, do or say that to another woman again! You treat women with respect! Understand me?" I pointed down at him.

"Oh my God. I can't take you anywhere," Bri said as she grabbed my hand and led me off the dance floor.

～

*L*ucas

"Whoa! Did you see that?" My best friend Danny laughed.

"Yeah. Poor guy. Do you think you should go help him?"

"Nah. He probably deserved it. That chick is one tough cookie."

"One tough beautiful cookie." I smirked.

I watched the other girl drag her to a table, and the two of them and a guy sat down. I'd assumed he wasn't her boyfriend or else he would have stepped in. I stared at her from across the club. She stood about five foot seven with an amazing body that was clearly visible through the tight dress she wore. Her long, wavy hair was a subtle brown with blonde highlights. She was very beautiful and sexy, and I couldn't keep my eyes off her, even though she just sent that man on the dance floor to his knees. The view to her was becoming less clear as people crowded around us and she disappeared from my sight.

"Let's go grab a drink from the bar," Danny said as he patted my shoulder.

We headed to the bar and Danny poured me a scotch.

"You've really outdone yourself with the club, Danny." I smiled as I sipped my drink.

"Thanks. It's been a long time coming. I can't believe it's finally open."

Out of the corner of my eye, I spotted the beautiful woman from

3

the dance floor walking up to the bar. As Danny was talking, my focus was on her.

"Dude, obviously you're into her. Go talk to her."

"So she can kick me in the balls?" I smirked.

He let out a laugh as he put his hand on my shoulder.

"I'll be right back," he said. "I need to go check something in the stock room."

As soon as he walked away, I turned my attention back to her. I stood behind her as I watched Cody hand her a glass of scotch. *Interesting.*

"Her drink is on me," I shouted to Cody.

I guess I was standing too close since her drink went flying all over my suit when she abruptly turned around.

"Oh my God." She placed her hand over her mouth. "I am so sorry." She grabbed a handful of napkins from the bar.

"Don't worry about it." I took the napkins from her and started wiping the scotch from my suit. "I buy you a drink and this is the thanks I get?" I spoke with a hint of irritation.

"Really? I'm sorry that you have a lack of respect for personal boundaries and were practically up my ass." She cocked her head. "I'll be more than happy to pay for you to get that five-thousand-dollar Tom Ford designer suit cleaned." She asked the bartender for a pen, wrote something down on a cocktail napkin and handed it to me. "Here's my phone number. Let me know how much it cost, and I'll Venmo or PayPal you the money. By the way, thanks for the drink."

She walked away and left me standing there speechless.

"Did she just give you her phone number?" Danny asked as he walked up next to me.

I stared down at the napkin and saw her name with her number. "Yeah. Apparently, she did."

～

One Week Later

"*G*ood day, Mr. Thorne."

"Hello, Kenny. Is my suit ready to be picked up?"

"It is. Let me go grab it for you."

Kenny was the owner of the dry cleaner my family had used for years. I remembered coming in here as a child with my nanny when she'd drop off my father's suits to be cleaned. Every time we would come in, Kenny would grab a lollipop from under the counter and lean over and hand it to me with a smile on his face.

When he walked over with my suit, he set it on the hook and rang me up.

"By the way, I found this in the pocket of your pants," he spoke as he handed me the cocktail napkin with Jenna's phone number on it. "I figured you might still want that." He gave me a wink.

"Thanks, Kenny. I appreciate it."

I walked out of the shop and handed my suit to my driver, Thaddeus.

"After you drop me at the office, can you run the suit home for me?"

"Of course, Lucas." He nodded.

As I was on my way back to the office, my phone chimed. When I pulled it from my pocket, I saw I had a text message from Sophia, one of the women I occasionally went out with.

"Hi. I'm sorry, but I have to cancel our date tonight. My sister is flying in tonight instead of tomorrow. I hope you understand."

Shit. I was really looking forward to getting laid tonight.

"Of course, I understand. We'll go out another time. Have fun with your sister."

"Thanks, Lucas. I'm available Tuesday night."

"I'll have to check my schedule and get back with you."

Damn it. Now what? I thought to myself. Placing my phone back in my pocket, I felt the napkin I had tucked in there before leaving the dry cleaners. Pulling it out, I stared at Jenna's name and number. Even though she spilled her drink all over my five-thousand-dollar suit, she

5

was still gorgeous, and I wanted to see her. The way she sent that guy to his knees and then copped an attitude with me saying I didn't respect personal boundaries intrigued me. I'd wondered if she'd have an attitude like that in the bedroom. There was only one way to find out."

CHAPTER 2

*J*enna

I was sitting at my desk when my phone chimed with a text message from an unfamiliar number.

"Hi, Jenna. I'm the guy you spilled your drink all over at the club. You gave me your number and told me to tell you how much the dry-cleaning bill was."

"Um, hi. I remember. Did you get it cleaned?"

"I did. In fact, I just picked it up. Instead of paying for the dry cleaning, have dinner with me tonight to make up for it."

I furrowed my brows as I read his message. I remembered the jerk and the attitude he gave me even though he was the one invading my personal space. But I also remembered other qualities about him. The sexy as sin physical qualities. Six foot two, great build, dark brown hair that was short and slicked back on the sides with a medium length textured top, penetrating brown eyes, and a strong chiseled jawline with a clean five o'clock shadow. What was the harm in having dinner with a sexy and handsome man? It was a Friday night, and I was available. The only plans I had consisted of pajamas, Thai food, and binge-watching Netflix. I enjoyed meeting new people. Maybe this time he wouldn't be such a jerk.

"Okay. I'll have dinner with you. What time and where?"

"Tavern on the Green at seven o'clock. I can pick you up if you'd like."

"That's okay. I'll meet you there."

"Excellent. I'll see you at seven."

When I arrived home, I threw my hair up in a messy bun and took a quick shower before I had to get ready to leave for dinner. While I was washing the dirt and grime off from the day, it suddenly hit me that I didn't know this guy's name. Ugh. How could I have been so stupid not to ask him. As soon as I finished my shower, I grabbed my phone and sent him a text message.

"Hi there, guy from the club! It's the girl who spilled her drink all over you because you have no respect for personal boundaries. You didn't offer your name and I totally forgot to ask you. So..."

A few moments later, he replied.

"We'll discuss more about personal boundaries at dinner, and I'll tell you my name when you arrive."

I stared at his message in disbelief. He was definitely a jerk and I couldn't believe I agreed to meet him for dinner. Maybe I should cancel. But I was hungry, and I loved Tavern on the Green. I'd just leave right after dinner. An hour tops with him. I could deal with his jerkiness for an hour. After putting on an "evening" look on my face and throwing a few curls in my long brown hair, I slipped into a short black dress with three quarter length flared sleeves. After zipping up my tall black boots, I grabbed my small black evening bag and headed to the restaurant.

I arrived at five minutes after seven, and when I stepped inside the restaurant, a perky blonde hostess greeted me.

"Welcome to Tavern on the Green. Dining for one?"

"No." My brows furrowed at her. "I'm meeting someone."

"Name for the reservation?" she asked.

"See, here's the thing. I don't know his name. He said he'd tell me when I arrived. He's incredibly handsome and has a lack of respect for people's personal boundaries."

"You're in luck. A handsome man just walked in about ten minutes ago."

"Did you get his name?" I smirked at her.

"Only his last."

"And?" I raised my brow.

"Thorne. Mr. Thorne. I'll take you to his table."

As she led me through the restaurant, I saw Mr. Thorne sitting in a corner booth staring at me. *Damn, he was sexy.*

"Good evening." He smiled as he stood up. "You're late."

"I was here. The hostess was trying to figure out whom I was meeting since I wasn't given a name."

"And she figured it out?"

"She did. I told her I was meeting a man who had little respect for people's personal boundaries. She knew instantly I was here to meet you, Mr. Thorne." I arched my brow as a small smile crossed my lips."

"You're cute." He smirked. "I'm Lucas Thorne, Jenna—?" I would shake your hand, but I don't want to get in the way of your personal boundaries."

"Larson. Jenna Larson." I extended my hand to him. "It's nice to meet you, Lucas."

"And you as well." He placed his hand in mine. "Thank you for agreeing to join me for dinner."

"Well, it's the least I could do since I did spill scotch all over your expensive suit."

"Good evening, Mr. Thorne. Madame." The waiter gave me a nod. "May I grab you a drink from the bar?"

"Good evening, Lorenzo. Scotch?" Lucas glanced at me.

"Of course." I smiled. "One ice cube."

"Two scotches. One ice cube for the lady and no ice for me."

"Very good, sir. I'll be back to take your order."

"I have to admit, I don't think I've ever met a woman who drinks scotch."

"What do you think that says about me?" I reached into the basket that sat in the middle of the table and pulled out a breadstick.

"I think it says you're very smart and you're not afraid to be different. I also think you're very independent."

"You're a smart man." The corners of my mouth curved upward.

9

The waiter delivered our drinks and took our dinner order. Picking up my glass, I gave it a little swirl and took a sip as he intently watched me. I felt as if he was turned on just as much as I was. He may have been a jerk, but all that was quickly falling to the wayside. He was gorgeous. More so than I remembered at the club. If he were to ask me to go back to his place, I probably wouldn't hesitate.

"I saw what you did to that guy at the club." A light smile formed on his lips.

"You saw that?"

"I think everyone saw that." He chuckled.

"Well, he deserved it for the things he said. I'm all for some dirty talk when it's warranted, but he took it upon himself to grind up against me without my permission, therefore, disrespecting my personal space. Plus, his line was lame."

"What did he say to you?"

"He said he wanted to take me out of the club and invade more of my personal space." I rolled my eyes and Lucas let out a laugh."

"You're right. That is lame. I guess he deserved what you gave him."

The waiter brought our food and set our plates down in front of us. As Lucas picked up his fork, his stare never left me.

"What?" I bashfully smiled.

"You're a beautiful woman, Jenna Larson. That's why I bought you that drink at the club. The one you so gracefully spilled all over my suit. And before you go on a tangent about how I have little respect for people's boundaries, the club was crowded and there were people all around that bar. I just squeezed into the closest space I could get because I wanted to meet you."

Maybe he wasn't a jerk after all. Maybe I had pegged him all wrong.

"Okay. Thank you for that." My lips formed a smile.

"You're welcome." He gave me a sexy wink.

CHAPTER 3

$\mathcal{L}$ucas

Not only was she sexy as hell and smart, but she also liked to drink scotch. I honestly didn't think a woman could be any sexier. My cock was throbbing as I sat at the table. It ached to be inside her, and I prayed to God she would agree to join me back at my place after dinner. All I needed was one night with her. One night to explore that gorgeous body under that dress. My cock started to rise at the thought, and I needed to settle it down.

"What do you do for a living?" I asked her as I cut into my steak.

"I work as a secretary for a small company."

"A secretary?" I arched my brow.

"Yes. Is something wrong with being a secretary?"

"No. Not at all. I just got the impression that you would be doing something a little more—I mean you seem—"

"Too smart just to be doing secretarial work?"

"Yeah. I don't mean to offend you, and I'm sorry if I did."

"No offense taken. When I moved to New York a year ago, I needed a job ASAP, and they happened to be hiring."

"So you're not from New York?"

"No. I'm from Massachusetts."

"May I ask why you left and came here?"

"There were a lot of reasons. One of those reasons is because my best friend lives here. She was still living with her mom, so we got an apartment together and agreed to split the rent and the bills. Then she met her douchebag controlling boyfriend and he managed to get her to move in with him."

"I take it you don't like him?" He smirked.

"I can't stand him. Bri, my best friend, is—how do I put this? She's weak in a sense that she can't stand up for herself. All she talked about was wanting to meet a man who worshipped her. She's dated some pretty douchy guys over the years, but Carson takes the cake. He's one of those men who singles out weak women he can control to make up for his tiny penis, and knows just the right things to say to make them fall under his spell."

"You sound like a man-hater." A small smile crossed my lips.

"I don't hate men. If I did, I wouldn't be having dinner with you. I just hate the ones who feel they're superior over women. Do you feel like that?" Her brow raised.

"No. Of course not. Do I give off that impression?"

"I don't know yet. I'm still trying to figure you out."

We finished dinner and I asked her if she wanted dessert before we left the restaurant. She said no, so I paid the bill and we left. As we exited the restaurant, I needed to make my move. But with this one, I needed to be careful or I'd end up on my knees holding my balls.

"It's a beautiful evening. Would you like to go for a walk in Central Park?"

"That's sound great and all, but I'd love another scotch. Know anywhere I can get one?" A seductive smile crossed her lips.

"I have a full bottle back at my place."

"Then let's go." She hooked her arm around mine.

"Let me call my driver and tell him we're ready to leave."

"You have a driver?"

"I do."

"I bet you live in a high-rise penthouse too." She glanced at me with a smirk.

"I do." I gave her a nod. "But I'm sure you already knew that since you called out my five-thousand dollar suit that night."

"Not really. Some guys like to pretend they're rich by wearing expensive suits, but in reality, they don't have a penny to their name."

I let out a chuckle. As Thaddeus pulled up, I opened the door and we climbed inside.

"Back to my place, Thaddeus."

"Of course." He gave me a nod through the rearview mirror.

~

*J*enna

It turned out to be a better evening than I thought. Mr. Lucas Thorne was charming and sinfully sexy. The scent that lingered from him was sexually enticing. I didn't remember that smell on him at the club. But it was the first thing that caught my attention when I sat down at the table. I leaned over as we were sitting in the back of the limousine and smelled his neck.

"What are you doing?" he asked with a confused look on his face.

"Shh. I'm concentrating. Fig, black plum, patchouli, coriander and a hint of leather. Very masculine." I smiled. "Must be Tom Ford's Noir Extreme."

"How—Are you some sort of men's cologne expert?"

"Nah. I just have a very sensitive nose. Were you wearing that cologne at the club?"

"Yes."

"Hmm. I mustn't have been able to smell it with all the other people there who were wearing perfume and cologne. Either that or you took a bath in it before meeting me at the restaurant."

"I most certainly did not! I dabbed on what I always do."

I started to laugh at how offended he was. We pulled up to his building and when he climbed out first, he held out his hand to me. Taking it, I stepped out and stood in front of the enormously tall building.

"I hope you don't mind heights," Lucas spoke as I followed him through the large glass doors.

"Good evening, Mr. Thorne. Ma'am," the gentleman in the navy-blue suit with the matching cap spoke.

"Good evening, Russell," Lucas replied.

"Good evening." I gave him a friendly smile.

The moment we stepped into the elevator, Lucas pulled a keycard from his pocket, inserted it and pressed the button to the 82nd floor.

"Oh come on. Really?" I asked.

"I warned you. But don't worry. Once you're up there, you won't even notice how high up we are unless you look over the railing on the terrace."

"Well, I won't be doing that."

He let out a chuckle.

As soon as the doors opened, I stepped out into a beautifully decorated foyer with light oak flooring.

"Wow. Wow. Wow," I said as I looked around the massive space. "How big is this place?"

"Almost five thousand square feet."

"And it's all one floor?" I asked as I followed him into the living area.

"Yes."

The entire penthouse was practically all floor-to-ceiling-windows. The cinematic skyline and river view was among the best I'd seen.

"What is it that you do for a living, Mr. Thorne?" I asked as I turned around and he handed me a glass of scotch.

"I'm the CEO of Thorne Technology Group here in Manhattan. My father runs our European office."

I swallowed hard. "Technology, eh?"

"Yes."

"Why is a sexy, good smelling, rich guy like you still single?"

"I prefer bachelorhood. I think it keeps life more interesting."

"Interesting how?" I threw back my drink to try and make me forget how high up we were.

"I don't think you want to hear my answer to that question. I may risk getting kicked in the balls."

"Tell me and I promise I won't harm your balls in any way." I gave him a smirk.

"I just feel a life-long commitment isn't right for me. I like my freedom. Relationships are hard work and I work hard enough as it is at my company. My work will always come before a woman and most women can't handle that. Plus, I want to avoid the emotional work necessary to sustain a fulfilling and intimate relationship."

"Okay. Fair enough. So basically you're a very selfish person who puts his needs before others."

His brows furrowed at me.

"I wouldn't say that."

"But you just did."

"No, I didn't."

"Yes, you did." I downed the rest of my drink and handed him my glass for a refill.

"What about you?" he asked as he walked over to his bar. "Why is a beautiful and sexy woman as yourself single?"

"You want the truth?"

"Of course." He handed me my drink.

"I'm single because I'm unique and it's not easy finding the right guy for me."

The corners of his mouth curved upward.

"Plus, I'm already a whole person and I don't need to find another half to complete me. Not to mention that I also love the casual sex where I can just walk away the next morning and go on with my independent life."

"Wow. Impressive." He threw back his drink and set his glass down. "You're a very beautiful woman and I'm completely turned on right now." He stepped closer to me and placed his hand on my cheek.

His lips softly brushed mine with caution while my lips went in for the kill. I was so horny for him, I thought I was going to die. As our passionate kiss continued, I unbuckled his belt and unbuttoned his pants while his hands unzipped my dress. In one swoop, he took my dress down as I kicked off my shoes.

"Damn." He shook his head as stared at me in my black lace push up bra and black lace thong.

Wrapping my legs around him, he picked me up and carried me to the bedroom as our lips stayed locked. Laying me on the bed, he hovered over me as he slid his fingers through the sides of my panties and softly stroked my vagina.

"You are so wet, and I've barely touched you," Lucas whispered. "Do you know how much that turns me on even more?"

"I suggest you show me how turned on you are."

As he stood up and unbuttoned his shirt, the only thing my eyes could focus on was his hard cock protruding through his black boxer briefs. The only thing my mind registered was "holy fuck." After he tossed his shirt on the floor, he took down his underwear. I gulped at how perfect it was. Big, but not overly large, straight, beautiful and lusciously hard. Reaching behind me, I unhooked my bra and tossed it over the bed.

CHAPTER 4

*L*ucas

She lay on the bed like pure perfection. I took my time and explored her entire body. I could feel the trembling of her skin as my tongue stroked her flesh. The subtle moans that escaped her when she orgasmed heightened my arousal. Her body shook with pleasure as I held her against me. Reaching into my nightstand, I pulled out a condom and slipped it on. She was more than ready, as was I. The anticipation of being buried inside her was killing me. I started at a slow pace for I didn't want to hurt her. She gasped as she took me in, inch by inch, until I was fully inside. I grabbed her wrists and held them over her head as I slowly moved in and out of her. The moans that escaped her lips were music to my ears. She orgasmed again and I asked her if she wanted more. She breathlessly told me yes as I pulled her up and she wrapped her long lean legs around me while I thrust in and out of her. My tongue slid across her neck as her hands slid through my hair and the warmth of her breath intoxicated me. She had me so worked up, I started to get rough and she welcomed it. She enticed it and I lost all control. I thrust in and out of her from behind like an animal. She screamed and begged me to go harder. The more she begged, the faster I moved until I couldn't hold back anymore, and I exploded inside her. She dropped down on the bed and my body collapsed with her. I struggled to catch my breath as did she and we lay there for a few moments until our racing hearts returned to their normal rate.

I pulled out of her and something didn't feel right, so I reached over and turned on the light.

"What's wrong?" she asked as she rolled over.

"Oh shit. There's a large tear in the condom!"

"No worries. I'm on the pill."

"You are?" I asked with a sigh of relief.

"Yeah. I have been for years. We're fine." She smiled.

I got up and went to the bathroom, removed the condom and threw it in the trash.

"I've never had a condom break on me before," I said as I walked back into the bedroom and pulled the box from my nightstand. "What the hell?"

"What?" She sat up.

"According to this box, these condoms expired over a year ago, and I just bought them yesterday."

"Don't you usually check the date before you buy them?" she asked.

"No. I guess I never really thought about it. I'm taking these back to the store."

"I hope you have the receipt."

I got up from the bed and pulled my wallet from my pants pocket. Looking inside, the receipt was folded and sitting amongst my cash.

"It's right here." I held it up.

"I know this is kind of awkward now, so do you want me to go?" she asked me.

"It's late. You might as well just stay until the morning."

"Thank God. I was hoping you'd say that. I'm exhausted." She laid back down, let out a yawn, pulled the sheet over her and closed her eyes.

Climbing in next to her, I reached over and turned off the light. The moonlight that filtered through the windows illuminated her as she laid in my bed.

~

*J*enna

I awoke the next morning as the sun shined through the windows. Grabbing my phone from the nightstand, I saw it was seven a.m. That had to be one of the best night's sleep I'd had in a long time. As I started to climb out of bed, Lucas stirred, and when I glanced over at him, his eyes were open and staring at me.

"Are you leaving already? You're welcome to stay for a cup of coffee."

"Coffee sounds good. Do you have any aspirin? My head is punishing me for how much scotch I drank last night."

He let out a chuckle.

"There's a bottle in the bathroom cabinet off the foyer. I'm going to take a quick shower and then I'll meet you in the kitchen for some coffee," he said as he climbed out of bed.

I watched as he walked his fine naked ass to the bathroom. Damn. He was amazing last night, and my body felt as if it was still trembling. As soon as I heard the shower turn on, I grabbed a t-shirt he had lying on the bench in his bedroom and slipped it over my head. As I walked to the kitchen, I took note of his entire penthouse. It was decorated in hues of beige with cream colored furniture that matched the light oak flooring throughout the place. The kitchen was simple but elegantly done with white oak cabinet and white marble countertops, including a marbled island that sat in the center with white oak matching bar stools. Over to the side, was a white oak round marble table that sat four with matching chairs. What really topped off the kitchen were the top-of-the-line stainless steel appliances and the Miele built in coffee maker. Thank God I knew how to use it because I was in desperate need for some coffee.

Once the coffee brewed in my cup, I grabbed it and walked over to the floor-to-ceiling windows where the sun filtered through and stared out at the city. Opening the door to the oversized terrace, I stepped out and looked around. It was decorated with outdoor furniture, an oversized barbeque and a table that sat six. Over in the corner, my eye caught the attention of the bubbling hot tub. I set my coffee cup down on the edge of the hot tub, pulled the shirt I was wearing over my head and slowly stepped in. Oh my God. This was exactly what I needed for my hangover. Picking up my cup, I relaxed in the hot tub while I sipped my coffee.

"There you are. I thought for a second you left until I saw your dress still lying on the floor."

"I hope you don't mind. I couldn't resist

"Not at all. You look sexy in there."

"Care to join me?" I gave him a sly smile.

"As much as I'd love to, I have some work I need to attend to in my office. Take your time and just let me know when you're leaving." He gave me a wink before walking away.

I really needed to get home and shower before I met Bri to do some shopping. Her douchebag boyfriend was playing golf today with his friends so he told her she could go shopping with me. When I was done with my coffee and using the hot tub, I dried off, went inside and slipped into my dress. Grabbing my purse, I found his office and stepped inside.

"I'm leaving. Thanks for the use of the hot tub and the coffee." I smiled.

"You're welcome." He got up from his desk and walked over to me. "I had fun last night." The corners of his mouth curved upward.

"So did I."

"I hope you understand that it was only what it was: a one-night stand."

"Of course I know that. That's all it was for me too. I better get going, I have some errands to run."

"Sure. It was nice to meet you, Jenna Larson." He pressed his lips against my forehead. "Take care of yourself."

"It was nice to meet you too, Mr. Thorne. Maybe I'll see you around sometime."

I walked to the elevator and as soon as I pushed the button, the door opened. Stepping inside, I gave him a small wave as the doors closed and I rode down to the lobby. When I got home and went into the bathroom to take a shower, I pulled my birth control pills out of the medicine cabinet to take it like I did every morning and noticed I'd forgotten to take yesterday's pill.

"Oh shit," I said out loud. I could have sworn I took the pill yesterday. But instead, I had taken some aspirin and forgot about the pill because I woke up with a bad headache. Popping both pills out of the pack, I chased them down with some water.

CHAPTER 5

SIX WEEKS LATER

*J*enna

My world had fallen apart, and I didn't know what to do. Not only did I lose my job because the two idiots I worked for didn't know how to run a company, but I also had thirty days to come up with the financing to purchase my apartment that was so conveniently being turned into condos. Whoever would pay to buy this dump was stupid and that was something I wasn't. To make matters worse, I had been sick with the flu all week.

"Maybe it's just nerves," Bri spoke as she sat next to me on the couch while I lay there wrapped up in a blanket. "Or maybe it's just the stress of everything going on. You'll find another job. It's only been a week. You know, Jenna, you can always—"

"No, Bri."

"But think of all the—"

"No. I'll have to find another apartment and a job."

"You know I would ask you to stay with us temporarily, but Carson wouldn't—"

I put my hand up. "I would rather live on the street than share a space with him."

"That's hurtful, Jenna." She pouted.

"I'm sorry, but you know how I feel about him and how he feels about me."

"I don't know why you two can't get along. I love you both and this really hurts me."

Suddenly, I could feel the vomit rising. Jumping up from the couch, I ran to the bathroom and hugged the toilet.

"Maybe you need to go to the doctor," she said as she stood in the doorway. "You've been sick for a week. Could you be—pregnant?"

"Oh my God. How could you even ask me that?"

"It was just a thought. Anyway, I have to go. I'm meeting Carson for lunch. Call the doctor. Maybe he can give you something. I'll call you later."

Pregnant? I swallowed hard. The thought never crossed my mind. Grabbing my phone, I sat back down on the couch and stared at my period app where I kept track of my periods every month. The weeks had gone by so fast that I'd forgotten about my period. Usually, I was reminded every month by the painstaking cramps I'd get a couple days before. But I hadn't had any of that. I tapped the app and sure as shit, I was late. But it had to be from the stress I was under. Losing my apartment, my job, not knowing what I'm going to do, and blowing through the little savings I had. I needed something to manage my stress, and maybe Bri was right about calling the doctor.

I was able to get into the doctor that afternoon after I told the receptionist I'd been throwing up all week and I thought I was dehydrated. I may have exaggerated a little bit just to get in. As I sat in the room and waited for the doctor to walk back in, I played a game on my phone to try and distract me from the nervousness that riddled inside me.

"I have your test results back," Dr. Levy said as he walked into the room and gave me a sympathetic look.

"I'm pregnant, aren't I?"

"I'm afraid so. You're about six weeks along. You have options, Jenna."

"I know." I looked down as I fiddled with my hands.

"I can give you the name of a good clinic if you're interested."

"I am."

He took a small notepad from his pocket and wrote the name of an abortion clinic down and handed it to me.

"If you decide to keep the baby, I suggest you get in touch with your OB/GYN and start prenatal care."

"Thanks, Dr. Levy," I said as I hopped off the table.

When I arrived back home, I called Bri and asked her if she would come over because I needed to talk to her. She thought she muted her phone, but she didn't, and I heard every word her and Carson said. She told him I needed to talk, and she was coming over. He said no and that he wanted her home with him, and he planned on them watching a movie tonight. I could hear the things he was saying about me and it took everything I had not to go over there and kick his douchebag ass.

"I'm sorry, Jenna. Carson and I have plans tonight. I can come over tomorrow morning before work."

"That's okay. We'll talk another time." I quickly ended the call before she had a chance to say anything else.

I was pissed, hurt, and full of rage. I needed my best friend during this turbulent time in my life and she couldn't stand up to her controlling boyfriend enough to be the friend she needed to be to me. That was the final straw as far as I was concerned, and I wasn't going to try anymore. As much as I tried to make her see she was in a toxic relationship, she wouldn't. But I was no longer going to be a part of it, so I considered our friendship over. I laid in bed all night and cried. I had no job, I was basically homeless, and I was pregnant.

The next morning, after tossing and turning all night, I pulled the piece of paper from my purse that Dr. Levy gave me and called the abortion clinic. I was in complete shock when the receptionist told me they had a cancellation and asked if I could come in at three o'clock. I agreed and tried to go about my day the best I could. Bri had sent me a few text messages, and I didn't bother responding.

I sat on the table in one of those hideous gowns as I swung my legs back and forth. Everything was happening so fast. I couldn't call my parents or even go back home. They'd told me once I left, there was no coming back, and I was no longer welcomed in their home or in their lives because I was nothing but a disappointment. But they were wrong. They were the disappointment, not me. No parent should ever treat their child the way they treated me. I placed my hands on my belly. What the hell was I doing here? This wasn't this child's fault. It didn't ask to be conceived, and I had no right to take its life away before it even began.

I jumped off the table and threw my clothes on. As I opened the door, the doctor was standing on the other side.

"Miss Larson?"

"Yes. I've changed my mind, and I'm leaving."

"Okay. That's good news. Take care of yourself."

"Thank you." I gave him a small smile as I ran as fast as I could out of the place.

I took a cab to Central Park so I could think. As I was walking through, I had to make a stop at the first trash can I saw and throw up. I was sure this wasn't morning sickness. Just nerves. Thank God I'd brought a bottle of water with me to sip on. Taking a seat on a bench, I thought about what I was going to do. I needed to find a new apartment and a new job ASAP.

CHAPTER 6

*L*ucas

I sat behind my desk and tried to figure out what the hell was wrong with the coding. My team had been working on the last half for the past six weeks and nothing. They couldn't figure it out either. I was in a multi-million-dollar contract and our deadline was approaching. The stress I was under was real. I'd barely slept and didn't have time to think about anything but this project. My father was up my ass about it, and no matter how many times I told him I was working on it, it wasn't enough. How could this even be possible? I was good, potentially the best, and I couldn't see where the error was. I only hired the best people, and they couldn't figure it out either. As much as I wanted my team to start from scratch, I couldn't ask them. We'd already been working on it for the last six months and the other work they had already suffered because of it. So, I decided to take it on all by myself.

I was in a foul mood when I stepped out of my office and told my secretary, Laurel, that I was leaving for the day and I didn't want to be disturbed at home. At least there, there wouldn't be any distractions and I could get a head start.

I arrived home at one o'clock and had already put six hours into it.

At seven o'clock, the doorman called and told me someone was here to see me.

"Who is it, Russell?" I asked.

"It's Jenna Larson, sir."

Jenna? What the hell was she doing here? I asked myself in confusion. I hadn't seen or spoken to her since our night together. I needed a small break any way, so I told him to send her up.

I waited at the elevator for her and when it arrived and the doors opened, she stood there gripping two extra-large suitcases.

"Jenna, what's going on?" I asked in confusion.

"I need a place to temporarily stay, Lucas, and you're my only option," she spoke as she wheeled her suitcases past me.

"What? What the hell are you talking about? Listen, Jenna. It's good to see you and everything, but this is a really bad time. I have a lot going—"

"And so do I!" she snapped at me.

"Okay. Let's both calm down and you can tell me what's going on with you. But I'm on limited time. I'm working on a very special project and I have to get back to it."

I walked over to the bar and poured us each a scotch. Her being here and trying to move in was the last damn thing I needed right now.

"Here." I held the glass out to her.

"No thanks." She put her hand up, and I gave her a strange look. "I'm pregnant, Lucas. I'm pregnant with your baby."

I stood there in shock as I felt the color drain from my face and the glass of scotch I was holding hit the ground.

"Ha! Same reaction I had." She grabbed hold of my arm and led me over to the couch. "I know you're in shock. Just give it some time and it will wear off. I'll clean that mess up."

I swallowed hard as a million little things raced through my mind. She was joking. She had to be. The thing was, she picked the wrong fucking night to pull this shit on me.

"You know what, Jenna. I appreciate a good joke every now and again, but this is not a good time."

27

"Joke?" She looked up at me as she wiped up the scotch from the floor. "You think this is a joke? I'm pregnant, Lucas."

"That's impossible! I know the condom broke, but you said you were on the pill!" I shouted.

"Yeah. I was on the pill, and maybe I messed the daily doses up. Who the hell knows!"

"How do I know the baby is really mine? For all I know, you could have slept with other guys right after me."

"Are you serious right now?"

"Yes. I'm dead serious. We slept together, I'm very wealthy and you see it as your opportunity to pin it on me for some quick rich scheme."

~

*J*enna

I blankly stared at him because I was in a state of shock by his words.

"You think I want any of your money?"

"Why else would you come here and tell me this?"

"Because you're this baby's father. I want nothing from you, Lucas. I don't even want you to be a part of the kid's life. I only came here because I need a place to stay for a few days until I can figure things out."

"And what happened to your apartment?"

"I had to leave because they're being turned into condos and I didn't have the money they wanted to buy it. According to them if you don't buy then get out."

"Surely you have money saved. Why wouldn't you go to a hotel? Better yet, what about that best friend of yours?"

"You know what?" I got up from the floor and threw the scotch-soaked paper towel in the garbage. "I'm sorry that I bothered you with this. And shame on me for giving you enough credit for thinking that you were a semi decent human being that I could count on for a few days. I won't bother you again." I grabbed my purse and my bags and rolled them to the elevator. As soon as the doors opened, I stepped inside and frantically pressed the button to the lobby.

I was so angry, I couldn't see straight. How dare he!

"Are you okay, Miss Larson?" Russell asked.

"No. I'm not. But I will be, Russell. Thank you for asking."

"May I help you with your bags?"

"No. I've got it." I gave him a fragile smile.

"JENNA, WAIT!" I heard Lucas yell.

"Leave me alone, Lucas. You said what you had to, and I'm leaving. You'll never hear from me again. That I can promise you."

By this time, the people in the lobby, as well as the workers, were staring at us as I exited through the doors.

"Just stop for fuck sakes." He grabbed my arm, causing a scene on the street. "Come back up to the penthouse. You can stay tonight. But I can't discuss anything. I have this project I'm working on and it's crucial I complete it."

I stared into his deep brown eyes.

"I'd rather sleep on a bench in Central Park than stay in your penthouse."

"Well, too bad. You're not sleeping on a bench in Central Park." He grabbed one of my suitcases and headed back into the building.

"Give me my suitcase back!" I ran after him, tripped over the threshold of the lobby doors and fell.

"Oh my gosh, Miss Larson." Russell ran over to me.

"Are you alright?" Lucas dashed over and knelt down next to me.

"Besides being completely humiliated? I'm fine." But I wasn't so sure about that.

Lucas grabbed a hold of my hand and tried to help me up. The moment I put pressure on my right foot, I screamed and fell back down.

"Let me take a look," Lucas said as he lifted my pant leg and removed my shoe. "Shit. You need to go to the hospital. It may be broken."

"Broken? Oh hell no. I'll be fine. Just take me upstairs. Please. I just need ice."

"Jenna. You fell and you said you're pregnant. You're going to the hospital."

"Fine. Russell will put me in a cab. You go back up to your project."

"No. I'm going with you. Just stay here. I'll be right back."

"Like I can go anywhere." I rolled my eyes.

"I'm so sorry, Miss Larson," Russell spoke sympathetically.

"Thank you, Russell. You're a good man. Unlike some."

While Lucas was gone, his driver Thaddeus walked into the building.

"Miss Larson, I'm here to help you to the car. It's best that I carry you."

"Yeah. No, Thaddeus. I'm humiliated enough. Bend down." I gestured with my hand.

He did as I asked, and I hooked my arm around him. As he helped me up, I made sure not to put any weight on my foot at all. The pain was unbearable.

"Okay. Let's go," Lucas said as he tried to wrap his arm around my waist from the other side.

"Don't touch me!" I pushed him away.

"It's okay, sir. I've got her," Thaddeus spoke.

He helped me in the car, and it took every ounce of strength I had not to burst into tears. I was so angry and scared. Not because of my foot. I could have cared less about that. I was scared for the baby. What if it got hurt when I fell? The most horrific scenes were playing in my mind.

"Are you—"

"Don't talk to me, Lucas." I put my hand up.

He let out a long sigh and turned his head so he was looking out the window.

When we reached the entrance to the Emergency Room, Lucas climbed out and grabbed a wheelchair while Thaddeus helped me out of the car and into it. Lucas wheeled me inside where we were immediately stopped by a security guard.

"How can we help you?" he asked.

"She fell and it looks like she may have broken her foot," Lucas said. "She's also pregnant."

"Follow me."

We followed him to the desk where a nurse who was about my age quickly took down my information.

"You say you're pregnant?"

"Yes."

"How far along are you?" she asked.

"About seven weeks now."

"Okay. Let's get you back there and make sure the baby is okay. Are you the baby's father?" She looked at Lucas and he hesitated to answer.

"He's having a hard time accepting it," I said to the nurse and she shot him a look.

"If you don't want him back there, we'll make him stay in the waiting room."

"I'm going back with you, Jenna. If you want to cause a scene, I'm ready."

I rolled my eyes at him.

"It's fine. He can come back with me."

We were immediately taken to a room, and I was instructed to change into a gown.

"What do I need this for?" I asked.

"The doctor is going to want to do an ultrasound to check the baby. Then we'll go from there."

"What about her foot?" Lucas asked. "Look at it. You can clearly see something isn't right."

"We will deal with that after we check the baby. Let me help you change into the gown," the nurse spoke.

"I can help her," Lucas said as he took a step forward.

"You can wait outside." I pointed towards the door.

The nurse let out a tiny laugh.

"Boyfriend?" she asked as she helped me take off my pants.

"One-night stand." I smiled.

"Ah. I see. He didn't harm you, did he?"

"No. I tripped walking into his apartment building."

"He's really hot."

"Yeah. It's about the only thing he has going for him."

She let out a laugh as she helped me lay down in the bed and put an ice pack over my foot.

"I think I love you." She grinned. "The doctor will be right in. Hang tight." She gave my hand a squeeze.

CHAPTER 7

*J*enna

Lucas walked back into the room and took a seat in the only chair next to the bed.

"You don't have to stay. You can go and get to work on your project."

"Just stop. I'm staying."

"This is your fault, you know," I said.

"My fault? How is this my fault?"

"If you wouldn't have said the things you did, I wouldn't have left and then I wouldn't have tripped running after your dumb ass trying to get my suitcase back."

"No. No way are you blaming this on me. You're the one who came to my penthouse out of nowhere and told me you're pregnant. No phone call, no warning, nothing. How the fuck did you expect me to react?"

"I knew you'd be in shock, but I didn't expect you to accuse me of sleeping with other guys right after you and saying the baby is yours to get money out of you. That isn't why I told you, Lucas."

"I'm not discussing this now."

"Hello there. I'm Doctor Reynolds, the OB/GYN on call." He walked over and held out his hand. "You must be Jenna."

"Hi, Doctor Reynolds."

"And you are?" He turned to Lucas.

"A friend."

"Huh. As if," I said, and he shot me a dirty look.

"So, you're about seven weeks pregnant and you took a fall." He looked down at my ankle. "Ouch. That definitely looks broken. But I'll send in the orthopedic doctor after we take a look at the baby. Because you're only seven weeks, we have to perform a transvaginal ultrasound. Have you ever had one done before?"

"No," I spoke with fear.

"It's no big deal. I'll have the nurse bring in the machine and we'll get started."

The nurse that helped me earlier rolled in the machine and got it set up.

"I'm just going to lower the bed so you're lying flat," Dr. Reynolds spoke. "Bend your knee with your good foot and leave the other one flat. We don't want you putting any weight on that foot."

He took the scope, inserted it into my vagina and looked at the monitor.

"Okay. Let's see what's going on."

I swallowed hard at the uncomfortable feeling, so I just put all my focus on the monitor.

"See this little peanut right here?" He pointed to the monitor. That's your baby and everything looks perfect."

Tears filled my eyes as I stared at the screen. I didn't know what Lucas was doing because I couldn't bring myself to look at him.

"The baby is fine, Jenna. So now we need to address that foot. Dr. Kensington is on call. I will go talk to him and he'll be right in. In the meantime, I'll have X-ray come down and get you."

"Can I have X-ray's if I'm pregnant?"

"Because it's your foot, the baby will not be exposed."

"Thank you, Dr. Reynolds."

"You're welcome. Take care of yourself and get plenty of rest."

As soon as the doctor and nurse walked out of the room, Lucas looked at me.

"I'm sorry, Jenna."

"I'm not discussing this now, Lucas. So you can just sit there and be quiet."

After I had the X-rays and saw Dr. Kensington, he confirmed my foot was broken and immediately put me in a fiberglass cast.

"You are not to put any type of pressure on that foot at all. You can either use crutches or a scooter. We'll send you home with a pair of crutches and if you feel more comfortable using the scooter, you can pick one up at the pharmacy."

"How long will I have to be in this cast?" I asked.

"A minimum of six weeks."

"Great." I sighed.

After I signed the discharge papers, I was free to leave.

"You're staying at my penthouse," Lucas said as he helped me from the bed and into the wheelchair."

"It'll just be for a couple nights until I can get some things figured out."

"We'll discuss that tomorrow."

When we arrived back at his penthouse, he took me directly to the guestroom where he put my luggage.

"I put you in the room closest to mine in case you need something. Change into your pajamas and climb in bed. I'll bring the bottle of Tylenol and a bottle of water."

"Please do not tell me what to do. But thank you for getting me Tylenol and water."

He let out a sigh as he left the room, and I unzipped my suitcase and dug through it until I found my nightshirt. I couldn't believe I'd broken my foot and had to stay in this stupid cast for at least six weeks. The doctor said because I was pregnant, my body would heal at a quicker rate. Shortly after I climbed into bed, Lucas walked in with a bottle of water and some Tylenol.

"Do you want to take a pain pill? The doctor said it's okay."

"No. I'm not taking anything but Tylenol. I'd rather be in pain than risk something happening to the baby."

"Okay. I'm actually going to head to bed myself. It's been a long day and night and I'm tired."

"I'm sorry I took you away from your project."

"Don't worry about it. I'll work on it tomorrow. Get some rest, and I'll see you in the morning. If you need anything at all, just holler. I'm right down the hall."

"I appreciate it, Lucas. Good night."

"Good night, Jenna."

CHAPTER 8

*L*ucas

I went to my bedroom and stripped out of my clothes. After putting on a pair of pajama bottoms, I poured myself a scotch and climbed into bed. It had been one hell of a night and nothing could have prepared me for it. I couldn't believe Jenna was pregnant with my child. Kids were never supposed to be part of my future. My entire world was crumbling before me. The project, the baby, and Jenna breaking her foot and having to stay with me. I wasn't sure how much more I could take before I lost it. Everything was at stake with this project and that had to be my only concern right now.

I had thought about Jenna over the past weeks since our night together. I thought about calling her on more than one occasion but figured it was best if we left it at a one-night stand. Seeing her again after all these weeks reiterated how beautiful she was, and the memories of our night together hit me like a ton of bricks. But that was all they were: memories. When the doctor did the ultrasound, I couldn't see anything, and nothing changed for me. I didn't want to be a father. I liked my life the way it was and nothing or no one was going to change that. I'd make sure both of them were taken care of financially, but that was all I could do. I wasn't ready, nor did I want to be a father. Perhaps I was selfish, but I couldn't help the way I felt. My work was more important and that was how it would always be.

The next morning, I climbed out of bed at six a.m. and walked to the kitchen for a cup of coffee. I had already planned on working from home all day so I wouldn't be interrupted, but now that Jenna was here, I was sure that wasn't going to be possible. When I walked into the kitchen, I glanced out at the terrace where I saw her sitting on the chaise lounge. After making a cup of coffee, I stepped out onto the terrace.

"Good morning. Why are you sitting out here so early? I thought the heights terrified you."

"Morning. They do, but I wanted to watch the sunrise."

"How did you sleep?" I asked as I sat down in the chair across from her.

"Not good. I was pretty much up all night in pain."

"The pain pill would have helped," I said as I brought the cup up to my lips.

"I know, but it's a sacrifice I'm making for my baby."

"What about your job? Did you tell your boss what happened and that you won't be coming in for a while?"

"I am currently unemployed."

"What? Why?"

"The two guys I worked for really didn't have a clue. When the investor pulled out, they were forced to close their doors. So, between losing my job and being kicked out of my apartment because I refused to buy it, you can see I'm kind of in a pickle. I never would have come here, Lucas, if I wasn't pregnant. But it's not just about me anymore. I only need a few days to get things figured out. After that, I'll be out of here."

"And where are you going to go with a broken foot?"

"I'll figure it out."

"What about your parents?"

"What about them?" She cocked her head.

"I'm sure they would help you out."

"Ha." She let out a light laugh. "They've pretty much disowned me."

"Why would they do that?"

"It's a long story and one I really don't want to get into." She picked up her phone and glanced at it. "I need to get inside. I'm not feeling well and it's about that time."

She grabbed her crutches and got up from the chaise lounge.

"It's about what time?"

"For the morning sickness to kick in. Just go about your day and forget I'm even here. I can take care of myself."

I got up and opened the door for her as she hobbled inside.

"I'm actually working from home today, and I can't be disturbed. I have some serious work to do."

"Don't worry. I won't bother you," she said as she went into the half bath and shut the door.

I couldn't bear to hear her vomiting, so I went to the kitchen and made another cup of coffee. As I leaned over the island with my cup between my hands, I thought about how she said her parents disowned her. What the hell did she do for them to disown their daughter? And what the hell did I get myself into? I really needed to be more careful who I chose to sleep with.

She hobbled back into the kitchen and asked me to grab her a bottle of water.

"Are you okay?" I asked.

"I will be in a few hours. I'm going to lay back down."

"Sure. Okay. I was thinking about bringing in a home nurse to help you."

"I broke my foot, Lucas. I don't need a home nurse and I can take care of myself," she said as I followed her to the bedroom holding the bottle of water.

"I just think it would be easier."

"On you?" She stared at me.

I wasn't going to lie to her.

"Yeah. I don't have time to—"

"Deal with me?"

"That's not what I was going to say, Jenna. Don't put words in my mouth."

"I'm really tired, Lucas," she said as she climbed back in bed.

"Get some rest. I'm going to take a shower and then go into my office to start working."

~

a few hours had passed, and I was getting nowhere. I stared at the large whiteboard hanging on the wall and rubbed the back of my neck. My phone rang and it was my father calling. Shit. I didn't need this right now.

"Hey, Dad." I put him on speaker.

"Lucas, have you made any progress yet?"

"I'm trying, Dad. I've been working non-stop and so has my team," I spoke as I headed to the kitchen for something to eat.

"One week is all we have left. One week, Lucas!"

"Don't you think I know that! I've been busting my ass on this."

"We cannot lose that account. Do you understand me? So you better work harder!" he shouted. "There will be severe consequences for you if we lose it. You promised me it could be done. You promised."

"I know, Dad."

"We're talking multi-millions of dollars. Figure it out, Lucas." Click.

I threw my phone across the island and when I looked up, I saw Jenna standing there.

"What was that about?" she asked.

"Nothing. Why are you in here?" I asked with irritation.

"Russell is sending up the delivery guy who's bringing my scooter."

"You ordered a scooter?"

"Yeah. I figured it would be easier and I can't stand these crutches."

The elevator dinged and when I walked over to it, a man stepped out and set the scooter down on the floor.

"This is for Jenna Larson," he said.

"That's me." She smiled as she hobbled into the foyer. "Do you have any cash for a tip?" she whispered in my ear.

Sighing, I reached in my pocket, pulled out a twenty-dollar bill and handed it to him.

"Thanks for bringing this over."

"Not a problem, man. Thank you."

"Look how cute it is," she said as she handed me her crutches. "I got the one with the basket so I can put things in it that I can't hold and scoot at the same time.

"That was a good idea." I smiled as she zoomed off across the floor. "That thing better not scratch up my floors."

"It won't. By the way, can I place a grocery order for delivery? You have no food in this place, and I want to cook dinner tonight as a thank you for letting me stay here."

"You don't have to do that, Jenna, but go ahead and get whatever you want. I'll go get my credit card then I need to get back to work."

CHAPTER 9

*J*enna

As I sat on the couch with my laptop and did some grocery shopping, I couldn't stop thinking about the conversation between Lucas and his father. He was under a tremendous amount of stress, and I wondered what the hell was going on and what the problem was with the project he was working on.

After the groceries were delivered and put away, I started dinner. Roasted chicken with twice baked potatoes and roasted vegetables. Lucas had been locked up in his office all day and I hadn't seen him since I walked in on the phone conversation between him and his dad a few hours ago. Just as I put everything in the oven, my phone chimed with a text message from Bri. I hadn't spoken to her in a couple of weeks, even though she wouldn't stop blowing up my phone.

"I went to your apartment to talk to you since you've been ignoring my calls and messages only to find out you don't live there anymore. I can't believe you stopped talking to me because I wouldn't come over that night. Everything doesn't revolve around you, Jenna. Carson told me to forget about you and that's what I'm going to do. Thanks for being such a shitty friend."

I stared at her message in disbelief as anger washed over me. It took everything I had not to throw my phone across the kitchen. So instead, I took a plastic spatula from the utensil holder by the stove and threw it, hitting Lucas as he stepped into the kitchen.

"Whoa. What the hell?"

"Sorry. I didn't expect you to walk in."

"Is something wrong, or do you just throw spatulas for the hell of it?"

"It's nothing." I gripped the edge of the marble island.

"Obviously, something is bothering you. I have a few minutes if you want to talk about it."

"It's just my ex-friend, Bri."

"The girl you were with at the club? The one with the controlling boyfriend?"

"Yes."

"What happened? Why are you calling her your ex-friend?"

"When I found out I was pregnant, I really needed her. So I called and asked if she would come over and her douchebag boyfriend told her no because he wanted her to stay home and watch TV with him. So, she told me no. She knew I had been sick all week with what I thought was the flu, and she knew I had lost my job and was being evicted. But she didn't care. She let that controlling freak tell her what to do. It was just the final straw. I don't need people like that in my life. Now she just sent me this text message." I handed him my phone.

"Wow." He handed my phone back. "That wasn't very nice, and I don't blame you for being upset. But don't let it get you down because you already have enough on your plate and the stress isn't good for the baby, or for you." He placed his hand on my shoulder.

"I know." I gave him a small smile. "I'm over it."

"Good. I have to get back to work. I can't believe you're cooking. You should be resting."

"Cooking keeps my mind off things. I'll let you know when it's ready."

"Okay." He walked away.

As I pulled the chicken from the oven, I heard the elevator ding, and it startled me. Scooting my way to the foyer, a man stepped out into the foyer.

"Why, hello there." His brows furrowed.

"Hi." I furrowed my brows back at him.

"Is Lucas home?"

"He's in his office."

"I'm sorry. You are?" He extended his hand to me.

"Jenna."

"Nice to meet you, Jenna. I'm Danny. What happened? he asked as he pointed to my cast.

"I fell and broke my foot."

"Ouch. You look so familiar to me. Oh my God." He pointed at me. "You're the girl who sent that guy to his knees at my club a few weeks back."

"Yep. That was me." I grinned. "I'm sorry."

"Please. Don't apologize. I'm sure he deserved it. Anyway, I'm going to head to his office."

"Okay. Dinner's almost ready. You're welcome to join us."

"As much as I'd love to, I'm afraid I won't have time. I just stopped by to check in on Lucas."

~

*L*ucas
    I heard my office door open, and when I turned around from staring at the whiteboard, I saw Danny.

"Hey bro." He walked over and gave me a hug.

"Danny. Hey. What are you doing here?"

"Just checking in to see how you're holding up. Um, care to explain the hot girl in a cast who's cooking dinner?"

I let out a long sigh as I rubbed my face with my hands.

"Dude, what's going on? I recognize her. She's the chick from the club."

"Yeah. She came over last night. She's pregnant with my child, lost her job and was kicked out of her apartment."

"What?" He laughed.

"I'm not kidding, Danny," I spoke with seriousness.

"Shit. You're going to be a father?"

"Title only as far as I'm concerned. Then last night, she tripped in the lobby and broke her foot. I was at the ER with her for over four hours. It's been nothing but one clusterfuck after another. I have her to deal with, this project that's miserably failing, and my father up my ass making threats if I don't get it fixed."

"Gee, bro. I'm sorry. Is there anything I can do?"

"Thanks. But no. I can't deal with anything other than this coding issue."

"You'll figure it out, Lucas. You always do." He hooked his arm around me.

"I'm not so sure this time."

After Danny left, I sat back down at my computer. Jenna had sent me a text message over thirty minutes ago that dinner was ready, and I lost track of time. Walking into the kitchen, I found her sitting at the table.

"I'm sorry. I lost track of time."

"It's fine." She snapped. "It's cold now so you might want to heat it up in the microwave."

"Don't get that attitude with me." I pointed at her with a stern voice. "I'm a very busy man and I didn't ask you to cook dinner for me."

"No. You didn't. I did it because I knew how hard you've been working, and you needed to eat. Sorry for caring."

"Nobody asked you to care, Jenna. You just need to understand how much pressure I'm feeling right now with everything, and frankly, I'm going to lose it very quickly here. So, I think it's in your best interest and mine, if you just did your own thing and let me do mine."

"Okay." She got up from the table, took her scooter and went to her bedroom.

I took my plate and put it in the microwave. Her attitude was the last thing I needed right now. When I finished eating the delicious meal she prepared, I decided to go and apologize to her. When I opened her bedroom door, she was sound asleep. I noticed she didn't have her foot propped up, so I took the pillow from the floor and carefully placed it under her foot.

CHAPTER 10

*J*enna

Since I had fallen asleep so early, I was up at five a.m. Scooting my way to the kitchen, I was shocked when I saw it was completely cleaned up. I had expected to do it this morning, but Lucas pleasantly surprised me. I made a cup of coffee and set it on the island while I went back to my room and grabbed my laptop. I couldn't stay here much longer, and I needed to find a job and a place. The more I thought about things, I knew what I had to do. Maybe I was just being rebellious to my parents. But now, I was going to have a baby and I needed to grow up and start adulting, the right way.

"You're up early?" Lucas said as he walked into the kitchen.

"I couldn't sleep anymore. Why are you up?"

"I need to get ready and go to the office. Are you going to be okay here by yourself?"

"I'm fine. Do you think I'm this weak fragile little girl that isn't capable of taking care of herself with a broken foot?"

"No. In fact, I think the complete opposite, but I just wanted to ask. Listen, I'm sorry about last night and I'm sorry for the way I spoke to you. It's just I'm under so much stress and pressure."

47

"What is up with this project you're working on?" I asked.

"You wouldn't understand." He sighed as he held his coffee cup in his hand.

"Try me."

"We signed a contract with a major company promising them something we can't deliver. When I proposed it, I thought we could. Now, multi millions of dollars are at stake and I have four days left to fix it or else I'm screwed. I honestly don't know what's wrong and neither does my team. We've been working on this for six months and we thought we had it right. My father is threatening me with consequences and putting more pressure on me."

"Then I come along with my news which adds even more pressure."

"Yeah. I'm not going to lie to you."

"I'm sorry, Lucas. I'm looking for a job today and I promise I'll be out of your hair soon."

"I can give you money, Jenna. I want to give you money to help you out."

"That's sweet, but I won't accept it. I don't take handouts. That's not why I told you about the baby."

"It doesn't matter. That's my kid and I'm responsible."

I looked at him as a small smile crossed my lips. "Technically yes, but to me you're not."

"I have to get ready for work. We still need to discuss all of this," he spoke as he walked out of the kitchen.

I felt for him. I really did. I could tell by his eyes and his face that he was exhausted and mentally drained. After he showered and dressed, he said goodbye and left for the office. After a couple rounds of morning sickness, I placed my hand on the knob of his office and opened the door. Stepping inside, I stared at the large whiteboard on the wall that was filled with coding and formulas. Making my way to his desk, I sat down, hit a key on the keyboard and the lock screen appeared.

"Shit."

Grabbing the notepad and pen that sat on his desk, I stood in front of the whiteboard and studied his coding. My knee was starting to hurt, as well as the excruciating pain in my foot from kneeling on the scooter, so I turned it around, sat down and propped my leg up on the sofa. Two hours later, I'd finally found something that didn't make sense to me. Scribbling formulas and codes on the notepad, I stared at it and something finally clicked. A wide grin crossed my face as I scooted my way to the bedroom, got dressed, grabbed my purse and took the elevator down to the lobby.

"Good afternoon, Miss Larson." Russell smiled.

"Hi, Russell. Please, call me Jenna. Can you get me a cab?"

"Of course," he spoke as he flagged one down.

"Where to, Miss?" he asked.

"This address please." I handed him one of Lucas's business cards I found on his desk.

When the cab driver dropped me off at the building, I scooted inside and looked around.

"May I help you, Miss?" A burly security guard asked.

"I'm looking for Thorne Technology." I handed him the business card.

"Fifteenth floor."

"Thank you." I smiled.

When I stepped off the elevator, I looked around at the hustle and bustle of people and was instantly stopped by another security guard who stood in front of me with his arms crossed. He was tall, overly muscular and bald.

"Can I help you?" His voice was deep.

"I'm here to see Lucas Thorne."

"Is he expecting you?"

"Um, no. But I have something I need to show him."

"Sorry, Miss. Not happening today. Mr. Thorne is very busy and doesn't have time for random people who just show up at his office."

"I'm not a random person, buddy. I happen to live with him!" I got up in his face.

"Come on, lady. Enough is enough. Step back into the elevator and go home."

"I'm afraid I can't do that. So please just give him a little call and tell him that Jenna is here."

"He gave strict instructions not to be disturbed."

I closed my eyes for a moment and took in a deep breath for I was going to lose my shit. Pulling my phone from my purse, I dialed his number and put it on speaker.

"Jenna? What's wrong?" he answered.

"Will you please call off your security dog and tell him to let me see you."

"What are you talking about? I really don't have time for this."

"I'm at your office, you idiot, and I need to see you. It's very important. The problem is this big guy won't let me through!" I spoke with gritted teeth.

"Why are you at my office?"

"I'll explain when I see you!" I spoke with irritation.

"Tell Andy I said it's okay and to bring you to the conference room."

I looked at Andy and smirked as I raised my brow at him.

"Follow me," he spoke.

I followed him to the conference room, and when Andy opened the door, I went inside.

"Thank you, Andy."

"No problem, boss."

"For fuck sakes, it's like a damn fortress in here," I spoke as I set my purse down on the table.

"What the hell are you doing here? You shouldn't even be out of the house. You need to be home resting!"

"I have plenty of time for that." I pulled the notepad from my purse and handed it to him.

"What is this? Is this the notepad from my desk?"

"Yes. I found the error as to why your coding isn't working. I rewrote it and I'm ninety-nine percent positive this will work."

"What?" His brows furrowed at me. "Jenna, this makes no sense," he said as he studied the notepad.

"It makes perfect sense, Lucas. Just put the coding in."

He took a seat at the end of the table where a large computer sat and began typing. After A few moments, his eyes widened.

"What the fuck!" he exclaimed. "It worked, Jenna!" A happy grin crossed his face. "Oh my God. It works! I can't believe this!" He placed his hands on his head. "How—" he looked at me from across the table.

"Long story for another time."

He walked over to me and gripped my shoulders. "I can't believe this. I just can't. I have a ton of calls to make and I have to bring my team in."

"And I'm going home to lay down. I'm exhausted."

"I don't know what to say but thank you. I'm at a loss for words, but we're going to discuss this when I get home." He kissed my forehead. "I'm going to walk you down to the lobby and have Thaddeus drive you back to the penthouse."

"I can get down to the lobby by myself. You just go do what you have to do."

"Are you sure? I can have Andy walk you down."

"Oh hell no. I've had enough of him for one day. I'm fine, Lucas. Just go take care of business." I smiled.

He pressed his lips against my forehead before we walked out of the conference room.

"Be careful. I'm calling Thaddeus now. You just go down and wait for him."

"I will. Good luck." I grinned.

He gave me a wink as he ran down the hall."

CHAPTER 11

*L*ucas

I was still in shock. How the hell did she do it? How did she know? My team was just as ecstatic as I was, but I didn't take the credit. I couldn't, and I told my team who Jenna was, minus the fact that she was having my kid. That was nobody's business, and I wasn't ready for anyone to know until I figured out exactly how things were going to go.

I left the office around five. Earlier than I normally did, but I needed to talk to Jenna. I stopped and picked us up some Chinese food for dinner. I didn't know what she liked, so I ordered a few different things. As I stepped off the elevator and headed towards the kitchen, I found her sitting on the couch with her foot propped up watching a movie.

"Hey." She smiled.

"I brought us some Chinese food." I held up the bag before setting it on the island. "I really hope you like Chinese."

"I love it. Thanks." She grinned as she got up from the couch and took a seat at the kitchen table.

I unpacked the bag, set the boxes of food on the table and grabbed a couple plates and silverware.

"I didn't know what you liked, so I just picked up a few different things."

"Actually, I love everything you got. Thanks. I'm starving."

"Didn't you eat today?"

"Not really. I spent the morning in your office figuring out what was wrong with the coding, met you at your office, and then I came home and crashed for about three hours."

"You need to make sure you eat."

"I know and I'm making up for it now." She smiled.

I sat down across from her and plated my food.

"And now we talk." I looked at her with seriousness.

"Yep. Guess we do." She looked down at her plate.

"Who are you really? Because I knew from the moment I met you, you weren't secretary material. You sat down and figured out why my coding wasn't working in a matter of what? Four hours?"

"Two." She glanced up at me.

"Okay. Two hours. You did what neither me nor my team could in the last six months. And let me tell you something, my team is one of the best."

"Obviously not." She bit into her egg roll.

I cocked my head as I narrowed my eye at her. She knew I was serious.

"Okay. Okay." She wiped her mouth with her napkin.

"My name is Jenna Larson, and I'm from Massachusetts. My I.Q. score is 165, and I graduated from M.I.T.

"165? Are you kidding me? 165 is at a genius level."

"Yeah. I know." I rolled my eyes.

"So let me get this straight. You're a genius, you have a degree from M.I.T. and you were working as a secretary making practically nothing? And you're homeless?"

"The pay wasn't all that bad. And actually, I have two degrees from M.I.T."

"Okay. Wait a minute." I set down my fork, got up from my seat and poured myself a much-needed drink. "What the hell are you doing? Why aren't you using your true potential to make something more of yourself? Do you have any idea the money you could be making and the lifestyle you could be living?"

"People treat you different when you're a genius. Some are ass kissers and users, and some are just pure evil and jealous. I've dealt with it my entire life. That's why I don't tell anyone about me and that's also why I choose to live a simple life. It's not about money for me, Lucas. It's about people and the relationships I form."

"And what about your parents? You said they disowned you? Why?"

"I was nothing more than a trophy they showed off. Everything revolved around my superior brain. When we'd meet people, they would introduce me as their 'little genius.' Not their daughter or by my name. Everything in my life was a competition, even if I didn't want it to be. I had to be better than all the other 'geniuses.' Science competitions, math competitions, physics competitions, swimming competitions. Every damn competition out there I was signed up for against my will. I just wanted to be normal. But I was robbed of a normal childhood. All I wanted to do was play outside with the other kids in the neighborhood. But I was forced to sit inside, studying and reading because that's what 'geniuses' did. I wanted to attend a regular school where the normal kids went. But that was out of the question because what kind of parents would they be if they sent their genius child to school with the unintelligent and mediocre kids."

"I'm sorry, Jenna. I had no idea."

"I didn't ask for this kind of intelligence and it sent me to some pretty dark places when I was younger. I was depressed, anxious, and practically suicidal at one point. My parents sent me to a therapist and I really liked her. I felt a connection to her. But when she mentioned to my parents that they were the cause of my issues, they made sure I never saw her again. After I graduated from M.I.T., I told my parents that I needed a break and I wanted to take a couple months off and travel around Europe with the money I had saved up over the years. They didn't like the idea, but they knew they couldn't stop me. I needed that time alone to really reflect on my life and to figure out who I really was behind the 'genius.' A couple months turned into a year. It was when I was in Italy that I met Bri. Her grandma lived there, and she was spending the summer with her. It was at the tail end of my travels, so I flew back to New York with her and then I rented a car and drove home to Massachusetts. I'd missed three interviews with large companies with a starting salary of $200,000 a year. My parents were livid, and my father told me I was stupid. A parent should never tell their child they're stupid, but to me, it was the best thing he'd ever said to me. After that, I packed my things, and they told me if I walked out their door, I was never welcomed back, and they would cut me off."

"When was the last time you spoke to them?"

"A year and half ago."

"After I left, I drove to Florida and stayed there for about six months and got a job working in the billing department of a car dealership. I wasn't really happy there and that's when Bri told me she was moving out of her parents' house and asked if I'd consider moving to New York and share an apartment with her. So, I sold my car to the dealership, hopped on a plane and here I am."

"Do you like it here in New York?" I asked her.

"I do. I really like it. And It's time for me to start adulting now that I'm having a baby."

"I can help you financially, Jenna, but in all honesty, I'm not ready to be a father." I downed my scotch.

"I know you're not ready to be a father, and I don't want your money, Lucas. I'm going to get a job. A real job with a company that's going to pay me a lot of money where I'm going to utilize my talents."

"But that's my kid too, and I need to help you out. At least monetary wise."

"You know, after I found out I was pregnant, I went to an abortion clinic. As I was sitting there on the table waiting for the doctor to come into the room, I really questioned what I was doing. I was taking this child's life before it even began and that would make me no better than my parents. The day they found out about my genius abilities, they took my life away from me. How could I do that to this baby? I'm going to have someone who's going to love me regardless. Someone who will still love me even when I make mistakes."

I gave her a small smile from across the table.

"Listen, Lucas. We've already established you're a selfish person and your work will always come before family."

"Really, Jenna?" I cocked my head at her.

"Yeah. Remember that conversation we had the night this little one was conceived?" She placed her hand on her belly as a smirk crossed her lips. "Anyway, I kind of like that you don't want to be involved. A child doesn't have to have two parents to be raised right. One of them would just end up screwing the kid up."

"I don't think that's true." I furrowed my brows at her.

"True or not." She shrugged. "I'm perfectly happy raising this baby alone. Besides, I'm a genius. How hard can it be? Anyway, thanks for dinner and I'm happy we talked and got everything out. I'm in some pain and I'm exhausted so I'm going to head to bed."

"Okay." I gave her a small smile. "I'll clean up. Good night, Jenna. And thanks again for your help. You have no idea how much it means to me."

"Good night, Lucas. You're welcome. I'm happy it worked."

CHAPTER 12

*L*ucas

I didn't know what to think. I knew she was smart based on our conversations, but I had no idea she was on a genius level. This posed a problem for me because she was exactly who I needed to work for me. But I wasn't sure if that was such a good idea.

After cleaning up from dinner, I decided to go to the club and talk to Danny. Before I left, I went to see if Jenna was awake

"You're up?" I asked as I poked my head through the door and saw her sitting up in bed watching TV.

"Yeah. I'm just watching a movie. What's up?"

"I'm going to run out for a while. Are you going to be okay?"

"I'm fine, Lucas." She smiled. "Go have some fun and celebrate."

"Can I get you anything before I go?"

"No. I'm good for now."

"Okay. Good night."

*W*hen I arrived at the club, I found Danny sitting in his office going over receipts.

"Hey, you." He grinned. "What are you doing here?"

"Just dropped by for a visit. I need to talk to you."

"Okay. Let's go grab a drink and sit at my special table."

I followed him out of his office, and he told one of waitresses to grab two scotches and bring them over to his table.

"What's going on, man?" he asked as we sat down.

"The coding is done and works perfectly. I'm meeting with Giles Holloway tomorrow to finalize everything."

"Alright, my man!" He grinned as he held up his hand for a high-five. "How did you do it? Did it just click or what?"

"Actually, I didn't do it."

The waitress walked over and set our drinks down in front of us.

"What? What do you mean?" His brows furrowed.

"Jenna figured it out, rewrote the program and gave it to me." I sipped my drink.

"Jenna? As in your baby momma with the broken foot who's staying at your penthouse?"

"Yep."

He let out a laugh. "Dude, what is she a genius or something?"

"Yeah. She is." I spoke with seriousness.

The laughter from his face fell as he stared at me.

"You're serious, aren't you?"

"Yes. I am. Danny, she has an IQ of 165 and she has two degrees from M.I.T."

"Damn, bro." He shook his head. "Then why is she staying with you?"

"Long story short, she doesn't like being a genius and wants to live a simple life."

"Genius problems." He rolled his eyes. "I wish I had those kinds of problems."

"I told her tonight that I could help her out financially, but I wasn't ready to be a father."

"Shit. What did she say?" He kicked back his drink.

"She said she knew and would prefer to raise the baby alone."

"Do you think she meant it or was she just saying that for your benefit?"

"Nah, she meant it. She's a very independent woman. But beneath all that independence, she's broken inside."

"Well, you know what? Congrats to you for impregnating probably the only woman in the world who doesn't want you around." He smiled as he held up his glass.

"Yeah. I got lucky." I tipped my glass to his. "I'm thinking about offering her a job at the company."

"Why the hell would you do that?"

"Because she's smart and I could use someone like her. Plus, she'd be competition if she were to go to work for another technology company, and I would be stupid to let her do that."

"I guess. But then she'd be in your life every day. You already said you're having nothing to do with the kid—wait a minute. Are you falling for her?"

"No." I frowned. "Of course not. This is purely a business decision."

"And if she doesn't want to work for you?"

"I'll just have to convince her she'd be making a mistake if she didn't."

By the time I got home, it was ten-thirty. After changing into a pair of pajama bottoms, I went into the bathroom and brushed my teeth. When I was finished, I was surprised when I walked out of the bathroom and saw Jenna sitting on the edge of my bed.

"Hey there. I thought you were sleeping."

"I can't sleep. Listen, we need to talk."

"Okay. What's wrong?" I asked as I walked to my closet.

"I'm incredibly horny."

I stopped dead in my tracks and turned around and looked at her.

"What?"

"I'm horny, Lucas, and something needs to be done about it. I mean, come on, you've already impregnated me so there's nothing to worry about. Plus, I consider us friends, and you owe me for fixing your coding problem."

The corners of my mouth curved upward as I walked over to her.

"I do owe you, don't I?" I said as I took a few strands of her hair between my fingers.

"The one time we had sex it was amazing, right?" She looked up at me with her beautiful eyes.

"Yes. It was amazing." I slid one strap of her nightshirt off her shoulder.

"Then there's no harm in repeating that amazing night. Do you agree?"

"I totally agree. I see no harm in it at all." I smiled as I leaned in and brushed my lips against hers."

"Thank God," she spoke as she wrapped her arms around my neck and pulled me on top of her.

CHAPTER 13

*J*enna

I gripped the sheets as he thrust in and out of me. Loud moans escaped my lips at the pleasure. I'd never forgotten that night we shared and neither did my body. My hormones were at an all-time high and I couldn't stop thinking about sex. Even while we were eating dinner, I couldn't stop thinking about his sexy body on top of mine.

"My God. I can't believe how wet you are," he spoke with bated breath. "This is incredible."

"It's a combination of your sexiness, skills, and my accelerated hormones. OH MY GOD! YES! YES!" I howled.

Lucas let out sexy sounds of his own as he exploded inside me and lowered his body on mine.

"Thank you," I whispered in his ear.

He lifted his head as the corners of his mouth curved upward.

"You're welcome. Are you good now?"

"I'm fantastic." I grinned.

He rolled off me and laid on his back as he tucked his hands behind his head. Propping myself up on my elbow, I stared at him.

"You reek of scotch," I said.

"I was talking to Danny at the club."

"Ah. Did you tell him everything worked out with the coding?"

"I did, and I also told him you were the one who figured it out."

"Why?"

"Because you deserve the credit." He smiled.

"That's nice of you, but you can take the credit, Lucas. I don't mind."

"Nah, I give credit where credit's deserved. Which brings me to something I want to talk to you about?"

"Okay."

"I want you to come work for me at Thorne Technology Group."

"I don't think—"

"If you're going to say that's not a good idea, that's where you're wrong. You need a job, I have one available, and I'll pay you well with full benefits. I'm guessing right now you don't have health insurance. Do you?"

"No." I sighed.

"That little trip to the ER is going to cost you a fortune, not to mention all the medical expense you're going to incur during your pregnancy. Now, please don't take this the wrong way, but I'm pretty sure no one is going to hire you with a broken foot and being pregnant."

I lightly smacked his chest.

"That's discrimination. They can't tell me I didn't get the job because I'm pregnant."

"No. But they would use your broken foot as an excuse if they wanted to. I'd hire you just the way you are." He grinned.

"Thanks." I rolled my eyes. "Let me sleep on it. I'm exhausted." I rolled over. "You don't mind if I sleep here, do you? I'm too tired to roll my way back to my room."

"I don't mind at all. Good night, Jenna."

"Good night, Lucas."

"I expect an answer tomorrow."

"Uh-huh," I spoke before drifting off to sleep.

He was sweet for wanting me to work for him, but I wasn't sure that was a good idea. Could he handle seeing me every day and my growing belly? My plan was to get a job somewhere else in the city, move out and move on with my life as a single parent. I was okay with that because I was independent and strong, and I didn't need a man to take care of us. My father always took care of my mother and wouldn't let her get a job outside the home. He said her duties as his wife was to stay home, raise the children or child, and take care of the house. She accepted that and seemed happy to do it. But I knew deep down inside a part of her wanted more out of life.

～

I stirred as I heard Lucas climb out of bed and get into the shower. Sitting up, I let out a long stretch and cringed at the throbbing pain in my foot. Grabbing my scooter and scooting my way to the kitchen, I made us each a cup of coffee.

"Hey, I thought you'd still be sleeping," he said as he walked into the kitchen with a towel wrapped around his waist.

"Couldn't sleep. My foot is killing me. I made you a cup of coffee. Just the way you like it. A splash of milk and one packet of stevia."

"Thanks, Jenna. I appreciate it." He smiled.

I sat down at the table and opened my laptop.

"What are you doing?" he asked as he walked up behind me.

"Business, Mr. Thorne. Can't a girl have a little privacy."

"Not if she's going to look for a job when she was already offered one."

"You do know it's too early to talk to me, right? Coffee first," I held up my cup, "talk after."

He rolled his eyes and walked out of the kitchen. After he left and I was in-between morning sickness, I submitted my resume online to two companies who had job openings that sounded like they would be the perfect fit for me. Within forty-five minutes, I received two phone calls asking if I would be available for interviews this afternoon. I sure as hell looked good on paper with my two M.I.T. degrees.

~

I was sitting out on the terrace with my foot propped up when I heard the sliding door open.

"You're home late," I said as Lucas took a seat next to me.

"I got tied up in a meeting. How was your day?"

"Meh."

"Just 'meh?'" he asked. "What did you do?"

"I went on two job interviews today." I glanced over at him.

"Really?" His brow arched. "That was fast."

"I look good on paper. Not so much in person."

"What do you mean?"

"They told me it wasn't feasible to hire me right now until my foot is completely healed, and they aren't even sure if the position will still be available."

"Hmm," he spoke.

"Don't say it, Thorne." I pointed at him.

"Well that sucks, because they lost out on an amazing employee. I, on the other hand, am willing to hire you pregnant, broken foot, and all." He grinned. "There's something else I need to talk to you about."

"What?" I sighed.

"I have an apartment for you."

"What do you mean? You went and rented me an apartment without consulting me?"

"No. I said I *have* an apartment for you. I own one of the apartments on the fiftieth floor. It was the apartment I lived in before I bought this one. The renters just called me today and they're moving out within the week because Mr. Taylor got transferred to the offices in Germany, and they need him there ASAP. So, I figured I'd rent it to you to go with your new job and all the money you'll be making."

"Is that so?" I arched my brow at him. "And you're sure I'll be able to afford the rent?"

"Trust me. You will be able to more than afford it with what I'll pay you in salary. It's a 1769 square foot three bedroom and two and a half bath. It comes fully furnished with a fully stocked kitchen of cookware, plates, glasses, coffee maker, silverware, bakeware, etc."

"Why didn't you sell it when you bought this place?"

"Investment reasons. We can go down and take a look at it right now if you want. The Taylor's are out of town but will be back tomorrow to start packing."

"Fine. I'll look at it."

The corners of his mouth curved upward. "Great. I'll go grab the key and we can go."

I walked inside the apartment on the fiftieth floor and took a look around. Beige and gray were the color scheme, and it was elegantly done. Solid oak flooring was spread throughout the apartment, except the bathrooms that were done up with a custom white Italian marble. I wouldn't lie. I really liked it.

"What do you think?" Lucas asked.

"I like it. It's nice."

"The views are great too." He walked over to the large, tall windows. You also get plenty of light in here during the day. So, what do you say? The apartment is yours if you accept my job offer."

"If I don't accept, you won't rent me the apartment?" I arched my brow.

"Nope. It's a two for one special." The corners of his mouth curved upward.

"Fine. I'll come work for you. When can I move in here?"

"Excellent. Mr. Taylor said he'll be out within the week. Then I need to get the painters and the cleaners in here. So, I'd say a couple weeks."

"Okay. I have a request."

"Of course. What is it?"

"I want new sheets. Preferably silk." I grinned.

"Done." He gave me a wink.

"When do I start work?"

"Tomorrow." He grinned.

CHAPTER 14

*J*enna

    I was in my room lying in bed and browsing the internet when Lucas walked in.

"Do you need anything?" he asked.

"No. I'm good. Thanks for asking." I gave him a small smile.

"Are you sure?" His eye steadily narrowed at me.

"Yeah. I'm sure."

"You absolutely don't need anything at all? Nothing? Not a thing?"

"No. I'm good." My brows furrowed at him. "Ah, wait. You're asking if I need sex."

"Jenna, I was not asking that."

"Yes, you were! Admit it!" I threw a pillow at him.

"Fine." He grinned. "I just thought I'd check before I head to bed."

"You're sweet for thinking about my sexual needs, but I'm good."

"Okay. Just so you know, I'm available if you have a sudden hormone surge or something."

"Good to know. Thanks, friend." I grinned.

"Friend, eh? Yeah. I guess we are friends." He smiled as he went to his room. "Oh, by the way," he said as he walked back and stood in the doorway. "You're only working half days at the office until your foot is fully healed. The other half of the day you'll be spending at home resting while you're working."

"You're the boss." I smiled.

~

Three Weeks Later

*J*t was my first night alone in my new apartment, and I was feeling a little down. It reminded me of the first night when Bri moved out. Even though I hadn't stayed with Lucas for very long, I grew used to him being around all the time. As much as I loved my alone time, it was still nice to know that someone would be walking through the door.

My job at Thorne Tech was going well. I liked it, and I liked the people I worked with. I even started to make friends with some of the men and women there. Everyone knew I was the one who saved the multi-million-dollar deal, but what they didn't know was that I was pregnant. I hadn't told anyone yet, and it wouldn't be too long before I started showing.

The next morning, as I was sitting in my office, Lucas walked in and shut the door.

"Do you have a minute?" he asked.

"Sure. What's up?"

He took a seat across from my desk.

"How was your first night in your new apartment?"

"It was good. Those sheets are amazing. Thank you." I smiled.

"You're welcome. Listen, Jenna, I've been thinking about something. You're going to start showing soon and I was wondering what you're going to tell everyone. I don't think it's a good—"

"If you're worried I'm going to tell people you're the father, don't be. I'll just tell them I had a few one-night stands, and I don't know who the father is. Let them think I'm a whore." I gave him a smirk.

"Jenna." An unamused look crossed his face.

"I'm kidding. I'll just say things didn't work out with the baby daddy and leave it at that. Your secret is safe with me, Mr. Thorne." I winked.

"Okay. I appreciate it."

He got up from his seat and walked to the door. Before walking out, he stopped, turned his head and looked at me.

"It was strange not having you around last night or this morning." He tapped on the doorframe and walked out.

A small smile crossed my lips as I looked down.

"Hey, Jenna." Lindsey smiled as she stepped into my office. "A bunch of us are meeting tonight at Rudy's for appetizers and drinks, and we want you to join us."

"Sounds like fun. Count me in."

"Great. We're meeting around six-thirty."

"I'll be there." I gave her a smile.

I wouldn't be able to drink, but appetizers I could definitely do. Plus, tonight would be as good a time as any to tell them about the baby and get the rumor mill around the office started.

~

When I walked into Rudy's, I saw my coworkers seated at a table.

"Jenna, over here!" Lindsey shouted as she waved her hand.

"Sorry I'm a little late. Traffic is horrible tonight."

"I'm heading up to the bar," Jake said. "What are you drinking?"

"Just water for me." I gave him a smile.

"Water?" Lindsey cocked her head. "Are you a recovering alcoholic?" She laughed.

"Recovering never. I love a good scotch more than I should sometimes. But I need to stick with water because I'm pregnant."

"You're pregnant!" Amara shouted.

"Oh My God!" Lindsey exclaimed. "Did you just find out? You never mentioned you had a boyfriend."

"I'm almost twelve weeks. I didn't want to say anything just in case—"

"Totally understandable." Amara grinned.

"Who's the baby's father?" Lindsey asked.

"This guy. Things didn't work out with us and I'm moving on."

"Aw. That's so sad," Amara said as she reached over and placed her hand on mine.

"Not really." I smiled.

"Here's your water, Jenna."

"Thanks, Jake. "Who needs a man in their life anyway?" I held up my drink. "No offense to you Jake. Or to you Cameron."

"None taken," they both spoke at the same time.

"Oh my, look who just walked in with the new flavor of the week," Lindsey said as she stared straight ahead.

Turning my head, I saw Lucas with some woman. Five foot five, long brown wavy hair and as skinny as an anorexic teenager. I quickly turned around as I sipped my water. What I wouldn't give to have a scotch in my hand at this moment.

"So, Jenna, does Mr. Thorne know you're pregnant?" Cameron asked.

"Yeah. He knows. I told him when he asked me to come work for him."

"By the way, how did you know about the project?" Jake asked. "That was top-secret."

"A mutual friend mentioned to him that I might be able to help out. So, he contacted me, and the rest is history." I smiled.

"What's it like being a total genius?" Amara asked.

"It can suck sometimes."

I turned my attention to the table where Lucas and the woman he was with were sitting, and he spotted me. Giving him a big smile, I waved at him. He slowly lifted his hand and gave me a small wave back. As I was talking with my coworkers, I noticed the woman walk by and head towards the restrooms. *I shouldn't. Yes, I should. Don't do it, Jenna. Do it, Jenna. You know you want to.*

"I'll be right back. I need to use the ladies' room," I told the group as I stood up.

Walking into the bathroom, I stood at the sink and waited for her to come out of the stall. When she did and walked over to the sink, I gave her a friendly smile.

"I love your dress," I spoke to her as I pretended to check my makeup in the mirror.

"Thanks. I love your hair. It looks so healthy."

"Oh my gosh. Thank you so much. I honestly think it's the prenatal vitamins I'm taking."

"You're pregnant?" she asked.

"I am. Almost twelve weeks."

"Wow. Congratulations. You and your husband must be thrilled."

"Oh. I'm not married."

"I'm sorry. I just assumed."

"It's fine. I got knocked up from a one-night stand and the father doesn't want anything to do with the baby."

"That's awful. I'm so sorry. Some guys are such assholes."

"It's okay. I'm totally fine with it. Besides, he's a billionaire and a kid doesn't fit into his lifestyle. Plus, he doesn't want anyone to know he's the father."

"Oh my God. What a jerk. Who is it? I promise your secret is safe with me. I know a few billionaires myself."

"I don't know." I slowly shook my head. "I promised I wouldn't tell anyone. But you seem like a sweet girl who can keep a secret. He's actually my boss."

"What?!"

"Right?" I arched my brow at her.

"Where do you work?"

"Thorne Technology."

"Seriously? Lucas Thorne is the father of your baby?"

"Yeah. He's my baby daddy. Do you know him?" I cocked my head.

"I guess I don't."

I could see the anger in her eyes.

"Please don't tell anyone. He'll kill me if he ever found out."

"Don't worry." She placed her hand on my arm. "I won't tell a soul."

I walked out of the bathroom with a smirk on my face as I sat back down at the table.

"Oh look!" Lindsey said as she gestured to Lucas's table. "Looks like Mr. Thorne won't be having a good night after all."

I glanced over and saw the woman grab her purse walk out of the restaurant in a huff. Oops. A moment later, I felt a hand grip my arm.

"Jenna, can I speak with you for a moment in private?"

"As much as I would love to get up and have a chat, I can't. My foot is throbbing since I got back from the ladies' room. Can it wait?"

I could tell he was angry, but he needed to keep his cool in front of his employees.

"Of course it can wait. Maybe you should go home if you're in that much pain."

"Maybe I should." I gave him a smile.

"Anyway, enjoy your evening everyone, and I'll see you at the office tomorrow." He shot me a look before heading out of Rudy's.

CHAPTER 15

*L*ucas

    I was pissed. I knew she said something to Melanie, and she had no right. No right at all. When I entered my apartment building, I took the elevator up to her apartment. Inserting the key, I stepped inside, took a seat on her bed and waited for her to come home. It wasn't too long before I heard the key slide into the lock and the door open. I could hear the wheels of the scooter approaching the bedroom, and when she flipped the light switch, she let out a shriek when she saw me sitting up on the bed with my back against the headboard.

"Jesus Christ, Lucas!" she shouted as she placed her hand over her heart. "You fucking scared me, you asshole! You just can't come in here whenever you feel like it."

"Sure I can. I'm your landlord."

"No you can't. You may only enter without permission from the tenant in the case of an emergency!"

"Well, this is an emergency. What the fuck did you say to Melanie?"

"Who's Melanie?"

"You know damn well who she is. She's the woman I was with.

Don't play games with me, Jenna. I saw you get up and go to the bathroom shortly after she did."

"I'm pregnant, Lucas. I pee non-stop. Besides, she wasn't right for you. She's a gold-digger. I could tell," she spoke as she took off her shirt and threw it on the bed.

"Really? And how do you know that?"

"First of all, half the women in New York are gold diggers. This is where the wealth is." She arched her brow at me. "The way you keep walking around in those expensive designer suits, the more gold diggers you're going to attract." She sat down on the bed and pulled off her skirt.

"I don't care. I'm not interested in anything but having a good time. You of all people know that."

"I suspect you brought her to Rudy's as a test because you knew she was a gold-digger, and I bet she moaned about it when you told her where you were taking her."

I looked away for a moment and sighed.

"I knew it." She leaned over and pressed her finger into my chest. "Honestly, she would have bored you, especially in bed."

She got up from the bed and I watched her scoot across the room to her dresser in nothing but her lacy panties and bra.

"Jenna, I'm warning you."

"Oh please." She pulled her nightshirt from her drawer.

I got up from the bed and stood behind her as I gripped her hips.

"I'm warning you. Stay the hell out of my personal life. Whom I chose to see is none of your concern," I whispered in her ear, and I could feel my cock rise.

"And whom I choose to see is none of yours," she said as I could feel her body tremble.

I slid my tongue across her neck as she tilted her head to the side and let out a light moan. My fingers unclasped her bra, and I took it off and tossed it on the floor. Grabbing each of her breasts, I gasped at the fullness of them. Her moans heightened as I took her hardened peaks between my fingers.

"I think you need to make it up to me for ruining my night."

"I guess I do. I've been a very bad girl."

I didn't think my cock could get any harder. After taking down her panties, I ran my fingers across her sensitive area. She was soaking wet and ready for me. After taking down my pants, I thrust into her from behind as her knee rested on the scooter. We both gasped at the pleasure as she gripped the edge of the dresser. Pounding in and out of her, she orgasmed quickly causing my cock to spasm with delight and I exploded inside her.

"Ah," I moaned as I pushed deep inside and pressed my lips against her bare shoulder.

When I was finished, I pulled out of her and pulled up my pants.

"I'll see you in the morning," I said as I walked out of her room and out of her apartment.

As soon as I stepped out of the elevator and into my penthouse, I poured myself a scotch and took it out on the terrace as I leaned on the railing and stared out into the brightly lit city. I wasn't sure if our friendship was working out. She had no right to do what she did, and it really pissed me off. After finishing my drink, I went back down to her apartment and knocked on the door.

"Hey," she said as she opened the door. "Is everything okay?"

"No. Things are not okay, Jenna," I sternly spoke as I stepped inside her apartment. "I think from now on we need to keep our relationship strictly professional. You're my employee and that's all you need to be."

"You're still pissed about Melanie, I take it."

"Damn right I am. You had no right."

"You're right, Lucas, and I'm sorry. It won't happen again."

"Damn right it won't. My personal business is none of yours. Do you understand me?"

"Yes. I understand."

"Good," I said as I walked out of her apartment.

~

*J*enna

I climbed into bed, and as I laid there, I thought about everything Lucas had said. What did I expect? A lifelong friendship with my baby daddy? A man who didn't even want to know his child, let alone be a father. Everyone had turned their backs on me, and he wasn't any different. If he was serious and wanted to keep our relationship strictly professional, then fine. Strictly professional is what it would be. I never should have agreed to work for him, but I felt as if I had no choice. I was desperate, and I had the baby to think about. All I needed was to get through this pregnancy. Plus, I couldn't stay in this apartment forever. It wouldn't be right running into Lucas all the time with the baby. This job was only temporary and after the baby was born, I would leave New York and move somewhere warm all year around, and I would buy a house on the beach for me and my child. Lucas wanting to keep our relationship strictly professional now sealed the deal for me. I felt a pain in my heart when I thought about him and our conversation earlier. Maybe I was wrong to do what I did, but there was a tiny part of me that was jealous.

CHAPTER 16

TWO WEEKS LATER

*J*enna

As I stood in the shower, I rubbed the bump that formed in my belly practically overnight. When I finished showering, I went to my closet and took out one of the skirts I wore to work. As I pulled it up to my waist and tried to button it, it wouldn't even come close. Shit. I struggled, and when I finally managed to get it buttoned, the button popped off and landed on the floor. I let out a long sigh as I tried to figure out what I was going to do. In the back of my closet was a grey jersey blend swing dress that I had bought over a year ago and only wore a couple of times. It would have to do for today. After work, and after my appointment to get my cast off, I'd have to go shopping for some new clothes.

I'd barely talked to Lucas the past couple of weeks. Whenever we did speak, it was nothing more than work related. He seemed a little cold towards me, and I didn't appreciate it. But if acting that way made him happy, then so be it. *Jerk.*

When I walked into the break room to grab a cup of coffee, I saw him standing at the counter pouring himself a cup. Walking over to the cabinet, I opened it and grabbed my mug.

"Good morning." He glanced over at me as he held the pot in his hand.

"Morning."

He poured some coffee in my cup and then looked me up and down.

"Is something wrong?"

"No. I've just never seen you wear that dress before."

"I know it's too casual for the office, but I had no choice. Nothing else fits me anymore." I placed my hand on my belly and showed him the bump.

"Ah. Looks like you need to go shopping."

"I do and I am," I said as I took my cup and walked out of the break room.

When I sat down at my desk, I looked up and saw Lucas leaning against the door frame holding his cup of coffee.

"Can I help you?" I arched my brow at him.

"I need you to be here all day tomorrow."

"Okay. Any particular reason?"

"My father is flying in tonight, and he'll be here all day tomorrow."

"Have you told him about the baby?"

"No. Of course not. He's never to know."

"Alright. My lips are sealed."

"Thank you." He gave me a slight nod as he turned and walked down the hallway.

I rolled my eyes the moment he walked away. His father was flying in. Interesting. I wondered why. I finished up what needed to be done before noon, grabbed my purse and headed to get my cast off. The cab dropped me off about a block away due to an accident that had traffic backed up beyond belief. I didn't care because I was getting this damn thing off anyway. As I was hobbling down the street, my eyes widened as I saw Bri coming towards me.

"Jenna?" She stopped when she saw me.

"Hey, Bri," I spoke in an uncomfortable tone.

"My God. How are you?" She reached over and hugged me.

SANDI LYNN

Breaking our embrace, she gripped my shoulders as she looked down at my belly.

"First things first, what happened to your foot?"

"I broke it. It's a long story."

"Are you pregnant? She placed her hand on my belly.

"I am." I smiled uncomfortably.

"I can't believe you didn't tell me. Why the hell wouldn't you tell me? Who's the father?"

Was she serious?

"I tried, but you were too busy letting your controlling boyfriend control you and our friendship," I spat.

"I'm sorry, Jenna. It's just—"

"It's just nothing, Bri." I started to walk away.

"I miss you!" She shouted.

"I miss you too. You can call me sometime when your douchebag boyfriend allows it." I walked away and headed to the building where the doctor was located.

❧

I walked out of the building feeling as free as a bird. Well, somewhat free. When I was out walking around the city or at work, I needed to wear a removable splint for a couple of weeks, which was fine. At least it was removable, and I didn't need it 24/7. After my appointment, I went shopping and bought some new clothes. As I was climbing out of the cab, and trying to gather the many bags I had, I heard a low voice behind me.

"Here, let me help you with those bags."

Turning around, my face was mere inches from a handsome older gentleman. He had salt and pepper hair that was slicked back, striking blue eyes, a light mustache and a salt and pepper beard that lightly graced his masculine jaw line. He stood about six foot three and wore a classy black designer suit. There was a familiarity about him. *No. It couldn't be.*

"Thank you, but I got it." I gave him a small smile.

78

"Nonsense. It's obvious we're going into the same building, so let me help you."

I sighed as I gave him a few of my bags and we walked into the building together.

"You've done quite a bit of shopping," he spoke. "I hope your husband doesn't mind." A smirk crossed his lips.

"I'm not married, and I would never marry a man who would have a problem with it," I said as we waited for the elevator to come down.

"Good." He smiled. "What happened to your foot?"

"I broke it about six weeks ago. I just got my cast off today and need to wear this while I'm out and about."

"I see. So you did a bit of shopping to celebrate?"

The doors opened and we stepped inside.

"No. I did some shopping because I'm pregnant and all my clothes aren't fitting anymore."

"Which floor?" he asked.

"Fifty."

He pushed the button to the fiftieth floor and then slid in a keycard and pushed the button to Lucas's penthouse. *Damn. I knew it.*

"You're pregnant?" he asked, and I swore I heard a bit of disappointment in his tone.

"I am." I smiled.

"Congratulations." He gave me a nod.

"Thank you."

When the doors opened on the fiftieth floor, I took the rest of my bags from him.

"Thank you for your help."

"You're most welcome. It's not every day I get to help a beautiful young woman." He gave me a wink.

"Somehow, I doubt that." I pointed at him as I grinned and walked down the hall to my apartment.

Wow. He was as smooth as his son.

CHAPTER 17

*L*ucas

"I want to meet the woman who figured out what you couldn't and almost cost this company a serious amount of money," my father spoke as we sat in the conference room going over the financial reports.

"She should be here in a few minutes." I let out a sigh. "I sent her a text message last night telling her to come straight to the conference room."

There was a light knock on the door, and when I looked up, Jenna stepped inside holding a coffee from Starbucks. My father turned around instantly a wide smile graced his face.

"You?" He grinned as he got up from his seat.

"Hello, Mr. Thorne. I'm Jenna Larson.

I sat there narrowing my eye at the both of them.

"Am I missing something here?" I asked.

"I had no idea." My father walked over, took Jenna's hand and brought it up to his lips.

"Your father helped me with my shopping bags yesterday when I arrived home," Jenna spoke.

"She certainly had a lot of them." My father smiled. "We must be paying her an awful lot of money."

"Well, considering her educational background, we are."

"I would love for you to join the two of us for dinner tonight," my father said to her.

Shit.

"Actually, I have—"

"Cancel them. I insist you join us."

"Alright. If you insist."

"Excellent. Lucas will fill you in on the details."

"Looking forward to it." She looked at me as she bit down on her bottom lip.

"You can get to work now," I said. "I'll drop by your office later."

"Okay. It was nice to officially meet you, Mr. Thorne."

"And you as well, darling." He smiled. "That one is a little spitfire," he said as he sat down across from me.

"Why do you say that?"

"I can tell from the brief conversation we had yesterday about shopping. Did you know she's pregnant?"

I swallowed hard as I could feel the beads of sweat starting to form.

"Yes. She told me before I hired her."

"She's not married, but I'm assuming there is a boyfriend."

"I don't know, Dad. She's just one of my employees. I don't know her personal life."

"I see. Well, that's the best way to keep employer/employee relationships."

After we finished going over the financial reports, I headed down to Jenna's office and shut the door.

"Hey," she said as she glanced up at me.

"You told my father you were pregnant?" I took the seat across from her desk.

"He asked me if I did a celebratory shopping because I got my cast off. I told him no, and that I was pregnant, and nothing fit me anymore. Don't worry. He doesn't know you're the father and he never will." She rolled her eyes.

"I have a feeling he's going to be asking you a lot of questions at dinner, so you better be prepared."

"Don't worry about me, Lucas. I can handle your father."

"Nobody can handle my father, Jenna. Dinner reservations are for seven o'clock at Daniel. Please try to be on time. If there's one thing he hates is when people are late."

"I'll be there on time."

I got up from my seat and headed towards the door.

"By the way, why didn't you tell me you were getting your cast off yesterday?"

"I honestly didn't think you'd care." She smiled.

"Fair enough. Why are you wearing that thing?"

"I have to for a couple weeks when I'm here or out and about. I don't need to wear it at home."

"That's good. I have to get back to my office. I'll talk to you later."

"Okay."

I went to my office and shut the door. Sitting behind my desk, I turned my chair around and stared out at the city. My father wasn't stupid and both she and I needed to be very careful with our conversations tonight.

~

*J*enna

After freshening up a few of the waves in my hair, I changed into a black short sleeve baby doll dress and slipped my good foot into a comfortable black flat shoe. As I stood at the elevator waiting for it to stop on my floor, the doors opened, and Lucas was standing there.

"Hey," I said as I stepped inside.

"Hey," he spoke as he stood there with his hands tucked tightly into his pockets. "You look nice."

"Thanks. So do you."

"Since we're leaving at the same time, you can just ride with me, I guess."

"That's okay. I have a cab waiting for me," I spoke.

"We're going to the same damn place."

The doors opened and I stepped out.

"Then maybe you should have offered that earlier today and I wouldn't have called a cab," I said as I walked away and out the lobby doors."

I climbed in the back of the cab and shut the door as Lucas stood there staring at me. I arrived at Daniel before he did and was taken to the table where his father sat.

"You look lovely, Jenna." He stood from his seat and kissed my cheek.

"Thank you, Mr. Thorne."

"Please, call me Lincoln."

Just as I sat down, Lucas walked over and shot me a look.

"Son. I'm surprised you didn't have Jenna drive with you since the two of you live in the same building."

"I suppose it slipped my mind," Lucas said as he looked at me.

"Well, I'm assuming it won't slip your mind to drive her home."

"No. It won't."

The waiter walked over and took our drink order.

"I'll just have water. Thank you," I said while Lucas and his father both ordered a scotch.

"So, Jenna, tell me about yourself," Lincoln said.

"Well, there's really not much to tell. I'm originally from Massachusetts, I graduated from M.I.T., and I moved here over a year ago."

"Which big company lured you to the fine state of New York?"

"Actually, I moved here because my best friend lives here."

"What about the baby's father?"

"Dad, come on. That's none of our business."

"We aren't together anymore. Things didn't work out between us."

"I'm sorry to hear that. How far along are you?"

"Almost seventeen weeks."

"Being a single parent is hard. I should know. My son's mother died during childbirth and—"

"Dad, that's enough!" Lucas snapped.

"Anyway, I trust you'll be able to handle it. You seem like a strong woman."

"Thank you, Lincoln. I'm not worried." I gave him a small smile.

After a stressful dinner, I said goodbye to Lincoln and climbed into the back of the car. Lucas slid in next to me and slammed the door shut.

"I think he suspects," he said in an angry tone.

"Why do you think that?"

"Because he's connecting all the dots, Jenna. I know my father."

"You never told me your mother died."

"Why would I?" He stared out the window.

"Your father raised you alone?"

"No. I had two nannies and servants that did a majority of the raising. The only thing he cared about was grooming me to take over the company one day. I feel like this is history fucking repeating itself."

"What are you talking about?" I asked.

"Nothing. I'm done discussing this."

~

I shoved my key in my purse and set it down on the counter as I took off my shoe. There were two sides to Lucas Thorne and that became clearer this evening. One side of him was a powerful rich man who had a caring nature when he decided to let it out. The other side of him was a frightened boy who never knew his mother and lived with a man he called his father whom he tried to please his entire life. But I got the feeling that no matter what he did, it was never good enough. I knew Lucas was damaged in his own way, but I didn't know to what extent. We were opposites. While he was trying to show his father he could be the best, I was showing my parents that I didn't want to be. I suspected he sought his father's approval for everything, while I sought my parent's disapproval.

At first when he told me he couldn't be a father I thought it was because he loved his bachelor life too much. That he was just a selfish man who couldn't be bothered. Maybe that was still the case, but after meeting his father and seeing the two of them together, I believed it was something much deeper.

CHAPTER 18

*J*enna

I was in the break room pouring myself a cup of coffee when Lincoln walked in.

"Good morning, Jenna. You're just the person I wanted to see."

"Good morning Mr.—Lincoln."

"I'd like you to join me for lunch today. I have a couple things I need to discuss with you."

"Okay. Will Lucas be joining us as well?"

"No. It'll be just us. Don't mention this to Lucas either. Understand?"

"Yeah. Sure. I won't mention it." I furrowed my brows.

"I'll meet you downstairs in the lobby at noon and we'll drive together," he said as he walked out of the break room.

I stood there leaning up against the counter as I brought my cup up to my lips. What could he possibly want to talk about?

"Morning," Lucas said as he walked in and interrupted my thought.

"Good morning."

"Is everything okay?" he asked as he poured himself a cup of coffee.

"Yeah. Everything's fine. Why?"

"You looked like you were in deep thought."

"I was just thinking about all the stuff I have to do." I gave him a small smile before I headed back to my office.

Looking at the time on my phone, it was eleven fifty-five. Grabbing my purse, I headed down to the lobby where Lincoln was already waiting. We climbed into the back of his limousine where he spent the entire ride to The Capital Grille on a business call. The moment we stepped inside the restaurant, we were immediately taken to our table.

"Good afternoon, I'm Clarissa, and I'll be waiting on you today. May I start you off with something to drink?"

"I'll just have water. Thank you." I smiled at her.

"And I'll have a scotch on the rocks, darling." Lincoln gave her a wink.

"So, to what do I owe the pleasure of having lunch with you today?" I asked as I picked up my menu.

"Maybe I just wanted to have lunch with a beautiful woman."

"Perhaps. But not today, Lincoln. Especially with a pregnant woman." I arched my brow at him.

He let out a chuckle as Clarissa set our drinks down and took our lunch order.

"Down to business. I like that about you." He took a sip of his scotch. "I know that child you're carrying is my son's."

I inhaled a sharp breath, and I needed to play it cool."

"What makes you think that?" I cocked my head at him.

"I'm not stupid or ignorant, Jenna. I can put two and two together."

"Then enlighten me, Lincoln."

"My son was very nervous last night. He was afraid you were going to slip after he told you not to tell me. Then there's the timing of you coming into the company. I pulled your file, and you were hired after you fixed the coding for the project my son was working on. The two of you had a one-night stand because that's all Lucas is in for, and you either got pregnant on purpose because you saw an opportunity, or my son was irresponsible. But in all fairness, I'm going with he was irresponsible because a woman like you and with your brain, you don't need a man to take care of you."

"You're right. I don't need a man to take care of me. I've been taking care of myself for a long time."

"Then there's the fact that he put you up in his apartment, which I'm to assume was to keep you close. Lucas isn't ready to be a father, Jenna, and he never will be."

I picked up my glass and took a sip of my water just as Clarissa set our lunch down in front of us.

"The truth will come out. I just wanted to speak with you first," he said.

He had me backed into a corner and this whole thing was stupid and a waste of my time. I wasn't playing these games.

"You're right, Lincoln. Lucas is this baby's father, and your grandchild. But we both had an agreement that he will have nothing to do with the baby and I will raise it on my own. I want nothing from your son."

"But you're working for our company and you rented his apartment. It seems like you want something."

"I was in a bind and he helped me out. You know what?" I set down my fork in disgust. "I saved that project for your company and this is how you treat me? You should be fucking grateful I did what I did. Lucas didn't ask me to do it. I saw it in his office in the penthouse and I took it upon myself to do something to repay him for letting me stay there after I broke my foot in his building."

"I am grateful to you, Jenna. Don't misinterpret that. But that's over and done with. Now we have a new set of problems."

"So you're saying my child is a problem?"

"I'm saying it's a problem if Lucas were to be involved."

"Why would that be a problem?" I cocked my head at him.

"Because when you feel, you stop thinking. And when you stop thinking clearly, everything goes to hell. Lucas has firsthand experience with that."

"Is that some bullshit line you've been feeding him his whole life? And what about his mother?"

"She was a woman I met and had a few good times with. She meant nothing to me. When she told me she was pregnant, I sent her to get an abortion. She couldn't go through with it, so I paid her off and she left town. Before she gave birth, she filled out some paperwork at the hospital listing me as the father and the emergency contact. When the hospital called to tell me she had passed away during childbirth and to come take Lucas home, I really didn't have a choice. I didn't plan on keeping him, but then I saw an opportunity to keep our family legacy going just like my father always wanted. But it stops with Lucas."

"You're a real piece of work, Lincoln. And I would never in a million years let my child be involved with your family. In fact, this baby won't even have the Thorne name."

"Good. That's what I wanted to hear. Lucas has enough responsibilities, and he doesn't need to add a child to the mix of things."

I pushed my plate away, wiped my mouth on a napkin and threw it on the table.

"Are we finished here?" I asked as I got up.

"I believe so."

"I'll take a cab back to the office." I reached over and grabbed my purse.

"Jenna?" He called out to me and I turned to him.

"I think you should reconsider working for Thorne Technology. As good as you are, I can't be having any distractions, and neither can Lucas. Name your price?"

"My price?"

"I will pay you a reasonable sum of money to get out of New York and never contact Lucas again. That way, you won't have to work, and you can solely focus on raising that child. You're a very smart woman and you know what the right thing to do is."

"Let me think about it, and I'll get back to you. I'm sure I can come up with a good number that will benefit us both." I turned and left the restaurant.

I thought my parents were horrible people, but Mr. Lincoln Thorne took the cake as far as parenting went. Now, everything was crystal clear where Lucas was concerned. He was merely a puppet and his father was the puppet master.

CHAPTER 19

*L*ucas

    I was heading to my office when I heard Jenna call out my name. Backing up and stepping into her office, I could tell she seemed off.

"What's up?"

"Can you come over after work? I need to talk to you about something."

"Is it really important? I have plans tonight with Danny."

"If it wasn't, I wouldn't be asking."

"We can't discuss it now?"

"No, Lucas. We can't. For fuck sakes, just forget it," she shouted.

"No." I sighed. "I'll come over. Watch that attitude, Miss Larson."

"When you watch yours, I'll watch mine." Her brow arched at me as she spoke in a snippy tone. "It works both ways, Mr. Thorne."

I couldn't help but smile as I shook my head and headed to my office.

I had a late lunch, so I wasn't worried about dinner when I stood outside the door of Jenna's apartment at seven p.m. After I knocked, she opened the door and I stepped inside. The smell of something enticing infiltrated the air.

"Are you cooking something?" I asked.

"I'm making baked spaghetti. It'll be done in a few minutes."

"I hope you didn't make that for me because I don't plan on staying."

"Sorry to burst your bubble, Lucas. I made it for me and the baby. We've both been craving carbs like crazy the past few days."

"Oh. What did you want to talk to me about?" I asked as I followed her to the kitchen.

She grabbed a glass of scotch from the counter and handed it to me.

"You're going to need this," she said.

I furrowed my brows at her as I held the scotch in my hand.

"You may want to sit down on the couch."

"For the love of God, Jenna. Just tell me whatever it is you have to tell me," I spoke in an irritated tone.

"Your father knows you're the baby daddy."

"WHAT!" he shouted as he fell into the stool at the island.

"I told you you'd want to be sitting down."

"How? How does—did you—"

"Before you start going batshit crazy," she held up her hand, "let me explain."

I threw back my drink and pushed the glass to her for another.

"Your father asked me to lunch today because he wanted to discuss something. I had no idea he wanted to talk about you and the baby. He backed me into a corner, Lucas. He put two and two together and figured it out. Let's be honest, he's a smart man and you really don't have to be smart to take a look at our situation and figure it out. By the way, your lecture is coming next."

"What? What the fuck does that mean?"

"He's going to confront you about it. I promised him I wouldn't tell you about our meeting. But, considering he's a vile and despicable human being, my word means nothing when it comes to him."

"What the hell did he say to you?"

"He told me to reconsider working for you and he gave me a lecture about you and how you're not ready and willing to be a father. I told him we agreed that I was raising this baby on my own, but that wasn't good enough for him. He wants to pay me off to leave New York and never have contact with you again."

"What did you tell that bastard?"

"I told him I'd think about it and I was sure I could come up with a reasonable amount that would benefit both of us."

"You are unbelievable," I scowled at her.

"If you really think I'm taking his money, then you don't know me at all. I'm playing the game, Lucas. I'm letting him think he has the upper hand."

"You're playing a dangerous game and you need to stop. You don't know my father."

"I know enough, and I know you feel trapped in the strings he has attached to you. Just like I did with my parents."

"You don't know what the hell you're talking about." I pointed my finger at her.

"Yes, I do. What happened in your past? Your father gave some lame line about if you feel, you stop thinking, and when you stop thinking, everything goes to hell. He said you have firsthand experience with that."

I swallowed hard as I narrowed my eye at her. Suddenly, I heard a timer go off.

"Hold that thought. I have to take the spaghetti out of the oven."

"Can you just forget about the damn spaghetti for a moment!" I yelled.

"Um. No. We're hungry!" I waved my hand over my belly. "Plus, if I don't take it out, it'll burn and create smoke which will set off the smoke detector and then the fire company will come out. Do you really want that? Because when they ask me what happened, I'll be more than happy to tell them that you demanded I leave it in the oven so we could continue discussing your piece of shit father!"

I stared at her as I clenched my jaw, unable to say a word.

"That's what I thought." She turned and opened the oven door. "You know, I thought my parents were bad, but your father—"

"Just stop. You've only known him for a couple days. I've had to deal with his bullshit my entire life."

"Care to talk about it over some baked spaghetti?" She held a plate up.

As much as I didn't have an appetite, it sure smelled delicious.

"Come on. You know you want some." She grinned.

"Fine. Just a small portion."

While Jenna took the plates over to the table, I grabbed the bottle of scotch off the counter.

"Why do you even have this? You better not be drinking."

"I stopped on my way home and bought it for you because I knew you'd be needing it."

"Thanks. I appreciate it."

"I'm sorry I told him the truth. I never would have if—"

"It's not your fault. I know my father and he always gets the truth out of people one way or another. I'm sure he manipulated the conversation."

"Pretty much." She nodded her head as she twirled some spaghetti around her fork.

"You didn't have to tell me, but you did. Why?"

"Because regardless of what you believe, I'm your friend, and I wanted to give you a heads up before he got to you. He never married, did he?"

"No," I spoke. "But there was never a shortage of women always coming and going."

"Reminds me of someone else I know." She smirked.

I let out a light chuckle.

"He's worse. When I was younger and did something he didn't like, he would tell me I should be grateful that he decided to keep me instead of putting me up for adoption. Sometimes, I wish he would have." I finished off my scotch.

CHAPTER 20

*J*enna

Little by little he was opening up to me. I felt for him because no child should ever have to hear those words. He was more broken inside than I originally thought. I guess we both were, which had me concerned for our child. Getting up from my chair, I walked over to him, grabbed his hand and led him over to the couch.

"What are you doing?" he asked.

I held onto his hand as I faced him.

"I'm going to tell you a little something about yourself and I want you to listen. Can you do that for me?" I gave him a small smile as he narrowed his eye at me.

"I suppose I could."

"Good. You have spent your entire life trying to get your father's approval. You want so badly to prove to him that he made the right decision by keeping you. You only buried your true self deeper by making choices based on the approval of him. In doing that, you lost who you really are, and you need to find out who the man inside you really is."

He looked away from me and inhaled a sharp breath.

"I didn't know you had a degree in psychology."

"I don't. But I don't need one to see what's really going on."

"And what about you?" he asked as he stared into my eyes.

"Me?" I laughed. "I spent my entire life trying to hide who I really was. We talked about that before. But I'm not hiding anymore. I'm letting people know who I really am and if they don't like it or can't accept it, they need to move on. The only approval I need is from myself."

He brought his hand up to my cheek as we stared into each other's eyes.

"You're a wise woman, Jenna Larson."

"I know I am." I gave him a small smile as he softly stroked my cheek and brushed his lips against mine.

It didn't take long for our kiss to become passionate as his hand wrapped around the back of my neck.

"I thought we were keeping things strictly professional," I spoke with bated breath.

"For tonight, we can forget that. Unless you don't want to?" He pulled back and looked at me.

"Oh no. I can totally forget that. In fact, I've already forgotten."

"Me too." He gave me a wink as he stood up and held out his hand.

Placing mine in his, he helped me up from the couch and led me to the bedroom where we spent the next hour making each other forget our troubles.

～

"You were a wild animal," he spoke as my head laid on his chest and his arm was wrapped tightly around me.

"Hormones, Lucas. Hormones."

He let out a chuckle. "I like your hormones." He kissed the top of my head and I couldn't help but smile.

"Are you staying the night?" I asked.

"I planned on it. Unless you'd like me to leave. But these sheets are amazing."

"Right?" I lifted my head and grinned at him. "The sheets and I want you to stay."

"Consider it done." He sat up, rolled me on my back and hovered over me. "One more round before we go to sleep?"

"Like you even need to ask." A wide grin crossed my lips.

~

*L*ucas

I lay there before the alarm went off and stared at her while she peacefully slept. A smile crossed my face as she stirred and opened her eyes.

"Good morning," I said.

"Good morning." She pressed her lips against my chest.

"The alarm is about to go off and I need to get upstairs to shower and change clothes."

"I know. Let me make us some coffee first and you can take it up with you."

When she climbed out of bed, she grabbed her robe from the chair. As she turned to slip it on, my eyes caught sight of the baby bump that I felt against me last night. I sighed as I climbed out of bed and slipped my pants on. Sitting on her nightstand was the book *What To Expect When You're Expecting*. Picking it up, I flipped through the pages.

"Coffee's ready." I heard her shout from the kitchen,

Grabbing the rest of my clothes, I took them to the living room, threw them on the couch and walked into the kitchen.

"Thank you."

"You're welcome. That look suits you." She grinned.

I looked down at myself and then back up at her.

"What are you talking about?"

"The whole pants and nothing else look. It's sexy. I like it." She slyly smiled as she leaned against the counter holding her mug in her hand.

"I can honestly say I like your look as well. A satin robe with nothing on underneath."

My cock started to get hard, and I let out a sigh. "I really need to get out of here and go shower."

"Shower here. With me." She bit down on her bottom lip.

"As tempting as that sounds, we'll be late for work if I do that."

She set her cup down and untied the strings to her robe, letting it fall open and exposing her naked body.

"Aren't you the boss?" She asked as she walked past me, and her robe fell off her shoulders and onto the floor.

"Damn it, Jenna." I followed behind her.

While the hot water streamed over us, I thrust in and out of her from behind as her hands were pressed firmly against the wall tile. Moans escaped our lips as the pleasure tore through us. Turning her around, I held her arms above her head as she brought one leg up to my waist. Holding her in place with my other hand, I thrust in and out of her, taking in the warmth she possessed inside. The second her body gave way to an orgasm, I buried myself deep inside her and exploded.

"Ah." I pressed my body against hers. "God, that was amazing."

"Yes, it was. Now we both can go about our day in fabulous moods," she whispered in my ear, and I chuckled.

~

The moment I walked into my office, I found a note on my desk that read:

I need to see you as soon as you decide to come in.
Dad

Sighing, I walked down to his office.

"You wanted to see me?" I asked as I stepped inside.

"You're late."

"By fifteen minutes. Traffic was horrible."

"I was in the same traffic and I was here on time." He leaned back in his chair.

Taking a seat across from his desk, I brought my ankle up to my other leg and made myself comfortable. I already knew why he wanted to see me, and I was ready, thanks to Jenna.

"Is there anything you want to tell me, son?" he asked.

"Not that I can think of. Why?"

"So you're not going to tell me that the baby Jenna is carrying is yours?"

"I knew you'd figure it out sooner or later."

"It's wasn't hard." He threw the pen he was holding across his desk. "How could you be so stupid, Lucas?"

"It was an accident, Dad. The condom broke and I didn't know it until after."

"So what are your plans with this kid?"

"Jenna knows where I stand as far as kids are concerned and she's raising the baby alone."

"What if she takes the baby and moves out of New York?" he asked.

"Even better."

He stared directly into my eyes trying to tell if I was lying or not.

"I cannot believe you let this happen. You obviously didn't learn from the last mistake you made."

I could feel the anger rising inside me.

"Accidents happen. You of all people should know that," I spoke in a smug tone.

"Don't get smart with me, boy." He pointed at me. "What are your feelings for Jenna?"

"Not that it's any of your business, but I don't have feelings for her."

"I highly doubt that. You took her in and let her stay with you when she broke her foot. Then you gave her a good job here, and you let her rent your apartment."

"She fell because of me, so I needed to do what was right. As for working here, I did it for this company because she's the best and we need someone like her on our team. As for the apartment, she needed somewhere to stay. What did you want me to do? Just let her loose on the street with a broken foot and nowhere to go?"

"Yeah. Why not? She's not your problem."

"She is my problem if she went to work for our biggest competitor. I was thinking about the company, Dad, and that's it."

He leaned across his desk and pointed his finger at me.

"You remember what I've taught you. When you feel, you stop thinking and when you stop thinking, everything goes to hell."

"I know." I looked down.

"You damn well better. I'm leaving tomorrow. Can I trust you'll be able to continue running this company without any distractions? I didn't keep you for you to fail me."

It took everything I had not to reach out and punch him in the face. Father or not.

"Yes. You can trust me."

"Good."

"Are we finished here. I have a lot of work to do."

"Yeah. We're finished."

I got up from my seat and headed to my office. Shutting the door, I took a seat behind my desk and let out a long sigh. Jenna was right. I could feel him pulling the strings he had attached to me. I needed to be alone for a while and away from the company and the city to think.

"Hey," Jenna spoke as she poked her head through the door.

"Hey. Come in."

"I need you to sign off on this," she spoke as she handed me a file folder. "Are you okay?"

"Yeah. I'm fine."

"It kind of looked like you were in a deep thought."

"My father called me into his office to let me know he knew about the baby."

"And?"

"He spewed his usual bullshit."

"Did you say anything back?" she asked.

"Not really. He's leaving tomorrow, and so am I."

"Oh. Good that he's leaving. Where are you going?"

"I just need some time away from here."

"How long will you be gone?"

"Probably a couple weeks. Can you make sure the company doesn't fall apart while I'm gone? Because where I'm going, I'll barely have service."

"Sure. I'll help keep an eye on things."

"Thanks, Jenna."

"Do you want to have dinner or something tonight before you go?"

"As nice as that sounds, I have to pack. I'll take a raincheck, though."

"Of course. When you get back." A small smile crossed her lips.

CHAPTER 21

ONE WEEK LATER

*J*enna

I hadn't heard from Lucas in a week. But then again, I really didn't expect I would. His trip was sudden, and I couldn't help but wonder if it had anything to do with our conversation that night. For his sake, I hope it did. I hated to admit that I missed him. I didn't want to miss him, but I did.

I lay on the table with my shirt pulled up while the nurse prepped the ultrasound machine.

"Are you comfortable?" she asked with a smile.

"Yeah. It seems as though lately laying on my back is the only way I can be comfortable."

"Just wait." She let out a laugh and placed her hand on my arm. "I'll go let Dr. Lewis know you're ready."

A few moments later, Dr. Lewis walked into the room.

"Hi, Jenna. How have you been feeling?"

"Hi, Dr. Lewis. I'm feeling pretty good."

"Excellent. No issues?"

"Nope. Not that I can think of."

"Then let's get started. Are you ready to see your baby?"

"I'm very ready." I grinned.

"If I can get a clear view, do you want to know the sex of the baby?"

"Yes. Definitely."

She squirted some gel over my belly and began moving the transducer around. As I intently stared at the monitor, tears sprung to my eyes as I saw my baby. I couldn't believe that tiny human was growing inside me, and a part of me wished Lucas was here to see it.

"Congratulations Jenna. It's a girl." Dr. Lewis smiled as she glanced over at me.

"Oh my gosh, a little girl." I grinned as the tears fell from my eyes.

"She looks perfect, and she's growing on schedule. I'll print out some pictures for you to take home."

As I walked out of the building, I couldn't help but stare at the pictures of my baby. Her facial features and her little body were perfectly clear. I could already tell she had Lucas's nose and my lips.

I'd done a lot of thinking the past week, and I decided to take a trip back home for the weekend to try and make amends with my parents. I wasn't sure how they were going to feel about the baby, but I would soon find out. My visit would go one of two ways: delightful or disastrous.

~

*L*ucas

I'd rented a lake house about an hour outside of Portland, Maine, from a nice older couple. It was beautiful, peaceful and exactly what I needed. The view of the lake was relaxing and visible from all sides of the house. I'd spent the last week doing absolutely nothing, and I didn't feel one ounce of guilt for it. I'd done some fishing, canoeing, and I hiked the trails near the house. But most importantly, I'd done a lot of thinking. Thinking about my father, my life, Jenna, and the baby. As much as I hated to admit it, she was right. I'd lived my entire life trying to get my father's approval. To make him see he'd made the right decision in keeping me, and that I was worthy. I was a thirty-year-old man still seeking the same approval and worth from him, and the cycle needed to stop. I had one more week at the lake house, and I was going to use it to my full advantage before I had to get back to the reality of life. A life I wasn't so sure of anymore.

~

One Week Later

*J*enna
I stood in front of the mirror and stared at my naked, expanding body. Now, it was more than obvious I was pregnant. It amazed me how fast the baby grew in the past two weeks. I had four months left to figure out what I was going to do and where I was going to go once the baby was born. I still hadn't heard a word from Lucas, and I didn't know when he was coming back. My visit with my parents went a little better than I expected. It was neither delightful nor disastrous. It was just fine, but it would take a lot of time if we were ever going to have a normal family relationship.

I was sitting at my desk working on an important project when I heard a light knock on the door.

"Come in," I said as I stared at my computer.

"Hello, Jenna."

Looking towards the door, I saw Lucas standing there.

"Hey. You're back."

"I am." He stepped inside and closed the door. *Damn, did he look sexy.*

Getting up from my desk, he noticed my belly and a look of shock splayed across his face.

"Wow. You really got bigger over the past couple of weeks."

"Yeah. It's real now." I grinned as I placed my hand on my belly. "How was your trip?"

"It was good, and very relaxing. I'm hoping you'll have dinner with me tonight. We need to talk."

"Sure. How about you come over, and I'll cook. That way we'll have more privacy," I said.

"You don't have to cook. I can bring something over. Is there anything you have a taste for?"

I stood there and thought about it for a moment.

"Mediterranean sounds good."

"Sounds good to me too." A light smile crossed his lips. "I'll stop at the place on the corner from our building, and I'll be over around seven. I have a lot of work to catch up on. Just text me what you want."

"I will."

He opened the door and stopped when I called his name.

"Lucas?"

"Yeah?" He looked at me.

"It's good to have you back."

"It's good to be back." He gave me a wink as he walked out of my office.

He seemed different. Calmer and relaxed. The pressures of life didn't show in his face like they had. I pulled up the online menu to the Mediterranean place and everything sounded so good. I finally narrowed it down and sent Lucas a text message with my order.

"Really? Are you going to eat all that?"

"Yes. Have you forgotten I'm eating for two?"

"Point taken."

CHAPTER 22

*L*ucas

After I left the office, I stopped and picked up the food and went up to the penthouse to change before heading down to Jenna's. The moment I knocked on the door and she opened it, she grabbed the bag of food from me.

"It's about time. I'm starving!"

I let out a chuckle as I stepped inside and shut the door.

"Can you do me a favor and take the food out of the bag? I have to pee," she asked.

"Sure."

"If you want scotch, the bottle is in the corner by the sink."

I grabbed the containers of food from the bag and when I went to pull out a couple plates from the cabinet, I noticed a picture hanging on the refrigerator. I took it off and held it in my hand as I stared at it.

"Did you—" She stopped when she saw the picture in my hand. "I was going to ask if you wanted to see it."

"When did you have this done?"

"A week after you left. Pretty cool, huh?"

"Yeah. It is." I placed the picture back on the refrigerator.

"The doctor said she looks perfect and she's growing right on schedule."

"She?" I looked at her.

"Yeah. It's a girl."

"Wow." I turned and took the plates to the table. "A girl."

"Can I pour you that scotch?" she asked.

"Please do and make it a double."

She set the glass of scotch down in front of me and took her seat.

"The reason I suggested dinner tonight was because I had a lot of time to think while I was away."

"Okay," she said. "But first tell me where you went." A smile crossed her lips.

"I rented a private lake house about an hour from Portland, Maine. It was beautiful and incredibly peaceful."

"Sounds very relaxing. What did you do besides a lot of thinking?"

"I did a lot of fishing."

She tried so hard to hold back the laughter but couldn't.

"I'm sorry." She laughed. "I just never figured you for a fishing guy."

"I never was, and I've only fished once in my life with Danny. But there's something to be said about being in the middle of a peaceful lake on a boat."

"I guess so." She pressed her lips together to avoid any further laughter.

"Okay. Okay." I smiled. "You had your fun. While I was on that boat everyday fishing, I did a lot of thinking about my father and about our situation. I think I'm ready to be a father."

"You think?" Her brow arched.

"I can't make any promises, Jenna. It's going to take a lot to undo the damage inflicted upon me by my father. I can't change overnight. But I will try to do my best. That's all I can give you right now. But I will promise I'll always be here for you. If you need anything, all you have to do is ask."

"I appreciate it, Lucas. But I'm fine on my own."

"I know you are, and that's what I admire the most about you. But you're my friend, and I'm here for you." The corners of my mouth curved upward. "I won't let you go through this alone. That's not the man I choose to be anymore."

"It sounds to me like you found yourself," she said.

"Like I said, I had a lot of time to think."

"I'm happy for you, Lucas. I truly am. Have you told your father any of this?"

"No. It's none of his damn business. Whatever decisions I make, are mine. I will no longer let him influence me."

"I'm proud of you." She smiled as she reached over and placed her hand on mine.

"Enough talk about me. Tell me what you've been up to the past couple weeks besides working."

"Actually." She picked up her glass of water. "I went and saw my mom and dad last weekend."

"Seriously?" I looked at her in shock. "How did it go?"

"They're excited about the baby. We did a lot of talking and there were a lot of tears. But for the sake of my daughter, I needed to make amends with them. I can't have any conflict in my life when she's born."

"I'm proud of you." The corners of my mouth curved upward.

"Thanks."

"You're welcome. I have a confession to make, and I just want to get it out of the way."

"Okay. Lay it on me." She grinned.

"I don't know the first thing about babies."

"Really?" She laughed. "That's your confession?"

"Yes. Why do you think that's so funny?"

"Because I already knew that. In fact, I'm pretty sure anyone who knows you knows that." She continued to laugh. "Don't worry. You're not alone. I don't have a clue about babies either."

"Are you scared?" I asked her.

"You bet your ass I am. I've never been so scared about anything in my life."

I picked up my glass and held it up.

"To us. Two scared friends who are having a baby and have no clue what they're doing."

Jenna picked up her glass and tapped it against mine. "And may we not screw up her life too much." She smirked.

"How are you feeling?" I asked her.

"I'm feeling good."

"I'm happy to hear that. And your hormones? Are they—"

"If you're asking if I'm horny, the answer is totally, definitely, and oh my God, yes!"

The corners of my mouth curved upward as I stood up from my seat and held out my hand to her. That was exactly what I wanted to hear.

"As your friend, I feel it's my obligation to help you out with that, if you don't mind. Remember, I'm here for you."

"I appreciate your kindness." She placed her hand in mine as I helped her up and led her to the bedroom. "My body appreciates it as well."

"It's my pleasure to help a friend in need." I gave her a wink as my lips brushed against hers.

CHAPTER 23

*J*enna

Lucas and I drove to the office together. He'd finally realized that since we both lived in the same building and were going to the same office, I should ride with him. He even gave me access to Thaddeus when and if I needed him. I was grateful for the new man Lucas had become, but I couldn't help but wonder how long it was going to last.

As I was in the breakroom pouring a cup of coffee, Lindsey walked in.

"There you are. I've been looking for you!"

"Why? What's wrong?" I asked.

"I cannot believe you lied to me."

"About what?" I asked in confusion.

"Who the baby's father is. You said it was some guy and things didn't work out. But come to find out, Mr. Thorne is the father. How could you keep that a secret?"

"I—I. How did you find out?" I cocked my head.

"He sent an email to the staff. You haven't seen it?"

"He what?!" My eyes widened.

"He sent an email telling us he's the baby's father and he just wanted to put it out there to clear up any confusion."

"It's complicated, Lindsey. You know him. He wasn't happy about it when I told him. But now he accepted it, and I guess he thought everyone should know."

"I didn't know the two of you were seeing each other. Nobody did."

"We aren't. It resulted from a one-night stand and we're just friends."

"Just friends?"

"Just friends." I gave her a small smile. "Am I forgiven?"

"Of course." She reached over and gave me a hug. "The whole office is buzzing. I just thought you should know."

"Oh well. Once the shock wears off, the buzzing will stop. I hope."

I walked down to Lucas's office and opened the door without knocking.

"Can I help you?" He smiled.

"What's with the email, Lucas? And who does that? Who sends an office memo to their staff telling them he's the father of one of his employee's baby?"

"Relax, Jenna. I just wanted to get it out in the open."

"You could have warned me first. The entire office is buzzing."

"They'll get over it soon enough."

Suddenly, I felt something in my belly that startled me.

"Oh my God." I placed my hand on my belly.

"What's wrong?" Lucas jumped up from his chair.

"I'm not sure. Oh my God." I felt it again.

"I'm taking you to the hospital," Lucas said.

"No, you're not. I'm not having pains. I think the baby kicked."

"Is that the first time you've felt that?" he asked as he walked over to me.

"Yeah. It is." I grinned as I took his hand and placed it on my belly.

We both waited patiently but nothing happened.

"Oh well. I guess she went back to sleep." I sighed. "I need to get back to work. I'll run down here if she starts kicking again."

"Good idea. Forget about the email and forget about the buzzing. Come tomorrow, it'll be old news." He kissed my forehead, and I narrowed my eye at him. "Don't give me that look."

"Then don't do things that make me give you that look." I arched my brow at him. As I turned and walked out of his office, I heard him chuckle.

∾

One Month Later

*L*ucas and I were the true definition of having a friends with benefits relationship. I did my thing, and he did his. We lived separately but had sex whenever we wanted. The only string that was attached to us was our daughter. Everything was perfect, or so I thought until one day I was out shopping. Pregnant couples appeared everywhere. Holding hands, kissing, and giving each other that look. The look of love, joy, and happiness. I felt like a pregnant fraud. Alone, unworthy and scared. Maybe it was the hormones. Maybe it was the fact that I wanted more in my life now. Or maybe it was because I'd fallen in love with Lucas, and I knew he couldn't return the favor. I couldn't tell him how I felt because I wouldn't risk damaging our friendship. I hadn't heard from Bri since that day we talked on the street. Obviously, she was still in the grips of her controlling douchebag boyfriend. If I tried to reach out to her, it would be the same old shit. I couldn't talk to my parents because they would tell me it was my fault for getting pregnant in the first place without being in a committed relationship. As much as I felt alone in this situation, I knew I wasn't the only single pregnant woman out there dealing with this.

After I left the baby boutique and five hundred dollars later on a few sleepers, I stopped by the electronics store to pick up a new laptop charger. As I was there, I overheard a woman tell her friend when they walked past me that she needed to get a better microphone for her podcast. Suddenly, a lightbulb went off in my head and a smile crossed my face. I could express my feelings to the world, and nobody would have to know it was me. I was high tech, and I knew exactly how to get a podcast up and running. After I purchased everything I needed, I went back to my apartment to set up my podcast which I called *Baby Drama*. I went by J. Elle, instead of using my first name because I needed to be careful. Being open and raw was how I was going to record, and I wasn't going to edit a single thing. What I said was exactly what people would hear. If anyone even listened to it. I didn't even care if anyone listened or not because talking about how I felt and what I was going through helped me. When I finished recording and speaking from my heart, I uploaded the content, shut my laptop down and went to bed.

The next morning, I slid into the back of the car and said good morning to Thaddeus. Lucas hadn't come down yet, and I was surprised. He was never late. A few moments later, the door opened, and Lucas climbed in next to me.

"Late night?" I arched my brow at him.

"Pretty much."

I couldn't help but wonder if he was with someone last night. He said he was going to JAMS to hang with Danny. A place where temptation was uncontrollable.

"I have a doctor's appointment this afternoon. Would you like to come with me?" I asked.

"I can't, Jenna." He glanced over at me. "I have a very busy day."

Disappointment shot through me because he'd never been to any of my appointments.

"Sure. I understand." I gave him a small smile.

"Maybe next time," he said. "How was your day yesterday?"

"It was good. I did some shopping and picked up some adorable sleepers from this cute little baby boutique over on Lexington."

"And what did you do last night?"

"Oh, not much. I just pretty much laid around and watched TV." I lied.

"It sounds like you had a nice and relaxing evening." His lips gave way to a sexy smile.

"It definitely was." I bit down on my bottom lip as I looked out the window.

I was sitting at my desk when I decided to take a small break from working and check my podcast stats. My eyes literally popped out of my head when I saw I'd already had over six hundred downloads and loads of comments in less than twenty-four hours. Listeners seemed to love what I had to say and they wanted more.

It was time to head out for my doctor's appointment, so I grabbed my purse and left. As I was sitting in the waiting room, I looked around at the four other women who were sitting there with their partners, and that feeling began to creep up inside me again.

CHAPTER 24

*L*ucas

"Mr. Thorne, your father is on line one for you," my secretary spoke through the intercom.

Rolling my eyes, I thanked her and picked up the phone.

"Dad, how are you?"

"I'm well, son. I wanted to let you know I'm flying back to New York in a couple days, and I've decided to stay."

A knot formed in the pit of my stomach.

"For how long?"

"I'm not sure yet."

"What about the Paris offices?"

"I put Jarod in charge. He's more than capable of keeping things in order here while I'm gone."

"Is there a reason why you're coming back?"

"Do I need a reason to come back to my goddamn company?" he snapped.

"No. You don't. I was just wondering—"

"You can stop wondering. I'll see you in a couple days." He ended the call.

Just what I fucking needed.

"Laurel, tell Jenna I need to see her."

"Of course, Mr. Thorne."

A few moments later, Laurel came over the intercom.

"She's not in her office, and I can't seem to find her."

"All right. Thank you."

Picking up my cell phone, I sent her a text message.

"Where are you?"

"At my doctor's appointment."

"Sorry. I forgot. Dinner tonight?"

"I can't. I have plans."

"Doing what?"

"I just have plans. Do I question you when you say you have plans?"

"Are you coming back after your appointment?"

"Yes."

"Come straight to my office."

She didn't respond. What plans would she have and with whom? I was pissed off as it was that my father decided to come back to New York, and now I was even more pissed that she turned me down for dinner tonight.

About thirty minutes later, Jenna walked into my office.

"You wanted to see me?"

I narrowed my eye at her because I could tell she was in a mood.

"My father called earlier to let me know he's coming back to New York and that he's staying for a while."

"Shit. Why is he doing that? And for how long?"

"I have no idea. Has he been in contact with you since he left?"

"No. I haven't heard a word from him."

"I guess we'll just have to see how things go when he gets here. That's all. I'm sure you have work to catch up on since you were gone."

"Yeah, I do." She turned and headed towards the door. "By the way, my doctor's appointment went fine in case you're wondering," she spoke with a serious attitude.

"Jenna—"

116

She walked out and shut the door. Leaning back in my chair, I let out a sigh.

~

*J*enna
"He wanted to go to 'dinner' and that also meant sex afterwards. As much as I wanted sex, I wanted to record my podcast more. Plus, he pissed me off by not having time to go to my doctor's appointment with me when I knew for a fact he didn't have any meetings scheduled. His promise to be there for me had faltered. But when said 'he'd always be there for me' what exactly did he mean? Perhaps it was my fault for not asking him to break that statement down detail by detail. Maybe doctor's appointments weren't included in the 'I'll always be there for you' statement. But dammit, is it too much to ask to go to a damn appointment? He'd already missed the ultrasound appointment when he was out in the world finding himself. These rollercoaster rides of emotions and hormones is exhausting. I'm a very strong and independent woman, but sometimes even the strongest have moments when they feel depleted, and that's okay. It doesn't make you weak or change who you are as a person. It only makes you human. We may think we're alone in our pregnancy, but we're really not. We have this beautiful baby growing inside that is with us 24/7. Talk to your baby. Tell him or her good morning when you wake up and tell him or her good-night before you go to sleep. But most importantly, have little chats throughout the day. So you see, we're not alone, and when we try to put our happiness into the hands of others either out of insecurity or fear, we are the only ones who suffer and fall victim to the pain when things don't turn out exactly how we want them to or expect they would. It's funny if you really think about it. The moment a woman decides to go through with an unplanned pregnancy, it gives the father a free pass to bolt. Remember, they aren't men. They're scared little boys who themselves have to grow up first, regardless of their age. One child to raise is enough. And as scary and tough as it sounds,

just remember, we women were made to do this, and we should feel honored and proud to have been given such a task."

I stopped the recording and uploaded the file. I hadn't checked my first podcast stats since early afternoon before my doctor's appointment, so I decided to check again before I shut my laptop down for the night. I had a total of two thousand fifty downloads and over a thousand comments.

Suddenly, there was a knock at the door. Closing the door to the second bedroom where I had my podcast equipment set up, I looked out the peephole and saw it was Lucas.

"Hey." I opened the door.

"Hey. Can we talk?"

"Sure. Come on in. Drink?" I asked him as I headed to the kitchen.

"Thanks, but no. I'm good."

"Okay. What's up?" I asked as I grabbed a bottle of water from the refrigerator.

"You seemed pissed off that I didn't go with you to your doctor's appointment."

"To be honest, I was."

"Why? Why would you be mad over something so insignificant as that? What would me being there with you accomplish when I could have been at the office doing more important things like work and making the company money."

Oh, hell no. OH, HELL NO. I took a moment to calm down before I threw my water bottle at him.

"Can you please define exactly what you meant when you said that you'd always be here for me?"

"What do you mean?" He shook his head.

"I need to know what that statement covers. Because I guess going to doctor's appointments isn't part of it."

"What the hell is wrong with you?" he snapped.

"Nothing is wrong with me," I spoke in a calm voice. "I just need you to clarify what falls under the 'I'll always be here for you' category."

"If you need me for anything, Jenna."

"Ah." I held my finger up. "For being so smart, I can be really dumb sometimes. The only thing that falls under that category is sex."

"That is not true!" His voice was stern as he pointed his finger at me.

"Well, I needed you there with me today!"

"For what?!" He held out his arms to the side.

"You know what? You are such a fucking typical guy."

"What the hell is that supposed to mean? You know what, Jenna. I don't need this right now. I have a lot on my mind, especially with my father coming back."

"You know what, Lucas, I don't need this either. I don't need the stress of you deciding when you want to be involved and when you don't. Just leave."

"Trust me. I am." He turned and headed towards the door.

"Good!" I shouted.

"You're crazy." He looked at me and shook his finger before walking out the door.

"Time to make a plan, little one," I said as I looked down and placed my hands on my belly.

After I changed into my nightshirt, I climbed into bed, put my belly buds on my tummy and played some Zen music for her. After hearing Lucas and I get into an argument, she needed some soothing and so did I.

"Alexa, play my Zen playlist."

I slowly closed my eyes and let the tension melt from my body and mind. Tomorrow was my first prenatal yoga class, and I couldn't wait. I probably should have started classes earlier in my pregnancy, but I couldn't because of my broken foot.

CHAPTER 25

*L*ucas
    I went back up to my apartment and immediately poured myself a drink. Taking it out on the terrace, I leaned against the railing and stared out at the brightly lit city. For her to get so upset about me not going to her doctor's appointment was absolutely ridiculous. I didn't need this shit from her. I had enough going on with my father coming back to town. I cared for her and the last thing I wanted to do was upset her, but she really pissed me off by saying what she did. We both just needed tonight to cool off and come tomorrow morning, things would be good again between us.

The next morning, I climbed in the car and looked at Thaddeus.

"Where's Jenna?"

"She told me she would be getting herself to the office from now on. Am I to assume something happened between the two of you?"

"She's just being childish." I sighed.

Before going to my office, I stopped by Jenna's and she wasn't there, so I walked into the break room where I found her making a cup of tea.

"No coffee this morning?" I asked as I stood behind her.

"You're being disrespectful of my personal space. Remember what happened the last time you did that? I would hate for that to happen again since I'm holding a cup of hot tea this time."

I took a few steps back.

"Better?"

"Much." She walked out of the break room and I followed her. "You're still mad at me for yesterday?"

"No, Lucas," she spoke as she set her cup down on her desk.

"Obviously you are."

She walked over to me and placed her hand on my chest as her eyes stared into mine.

"What happened last night is done and over with. We both had our say and it's in the past. Let's leave it there. I'm not mad."

"I don't believe you."

"Then that's your problem." She took a seat behind her desk.

"If you're no longer mad, have dinner with me tonight."

"I can't." She looked up at me.

"Why not?"

"Because I have a prenatal yoga class."

"A prenatal yoga class. Since when?"

"Tonight is my first class."

"Then we're having lunch. I'll pick you up at noon." I walked out of her office.

We ended up at The Capital Grille because Jenna was craving their signature burger and truffle fries. The moment we sat down, she ordered a water and some hot tea while I ordered a scotch.

"How did your doctor's appointment go yesterday?" I asked with caution.

"I told you yesterday it went fine."

"Listen, Jenna. I apologize. Okay? I didn't realize it was that important to you that I be there. I promise I'll go with you to the next appointment."

"It's fine, Lucas. Let's just forget about it. Like you said, you have enough to worry about with your father coming back to town. I have to pee. I'll be right back."

"Here's your scotch and your wife's tea and water," the waitress spoke.

"She's not my wife." I immediately corrected her.

"Oh. I'm sorry. Are you ready to order or do you want to wait until your girlfriend gets back?"

I let out a sigh.

"She's not my girlfriend either. Just because a man and a woman are having lunch together doesn't mean they're a couple. And yes, we're ready to order. We'll both have the signature burger with everything on it and the truffle fries."

"I'll get that in right away, and I'm sorry for assuming."

Jenna walked back to the table and sat down.

"I ordered our lunch."

"Thanks. I'm starving. Why is there not a bread basket on the table?"

"I think you only get that at dinner." I smirked. "We really haven't talked much the past week. How have you been feeling?"

"Good." She picked up her glass of water.

"Just good?" I asked because she was being vague.

"Yeah." She smiled.

The waitress walked over and set our plates down in front of us.

"Thank God. I'm starving!" Jenna said as she shoved a fry in her mouth.

"How far along are you?" The waitress asked her.

"Twenty-four weeks."

"I'm fifteen weeks." The waitress placed her hand on her small belly, and I sighed.

"Congratulations. You're so tiny still." Jenna grinned. "But just wait. One morning you're going to wake up and that belly will be popped out."

"I can't wait. Anyway, enjoy your lunch."

"Did that make you uncomfortable?" She cocked her head at me.

"It was a little weird. Don't you think?"

"Not at all." She took a big bite of her burger. "It's no different than you boys talking about your penis size."

"Really? We do not do that."

"I think you do." She scrunched her face. "In fact, I know you do. One time, I was sitting in a bar and there were two guys next to me and that's all they talked about." She shoved a fry in her mouth.

I just sat there and shook my head at her.

"What? It's true." She smiled.

"What time is your yoga class tonight?"

"It's from seven until eight."

"Why don't you come up to the penthouse tonight. It's been a while."

"I don't know. I might be too sore after yoga."

"Then let me do all the work." I gave her a smirk. "You know I'm good with my hands. I can make all your soreness go away.

"Okay. I'll come up after I shower."

"Good." I gave her a wink.

~

*J*enna

Before we left the restaurant, I had to pee again, so I told Lucas I'd meet him in the car. As I was washing my hands, the waitress that served us walked in.

"I just have to ask you something before you leave," she said.

"Of course."

"Are you J. Elle?"

Shit. How did she know?

"How did you know?"

"When you were in here earlier, the guy you're with told me that you're not his wife or his girlfriend when I mentioned it, and when you told me how many weeks you were, I just put two and two together. I just love your podcast. You have no idea how much you've helped me so far. When my boyfriend found out I was pregnant, he took off and said he wasn't ready to be a father. I'm twenty-one years old and I'm scared shitless to raise this baby on my own. But after listening to your two podcasts, I don't know. I just feel more confident now and empowered."

"Aw." I reached over and hugged her. "Thank you."

"No. Thank you. Please keep doing what you're doing. I've read all the comments and you're helping so many single pregnant women."

"You have totally made my day—"

"Natalie." She smiled.

"Natalie. You are a strong woman, and you got this girl."

"I know." She looked down.

"Listen, I have to run. He's waiting for me in the car."

"He's kind of a jerk," she said, and I let out a laugh.

"Yeah. He can be."

When I climbed into the car, Lucas looked at me.

"What the hell took you so long?"

"Ask your daughter." I cocked my head at him.

CHAPTER 26

ONE WEEK LATER

*L*ucas

Tomorrow was the day my father was blowing into town. Something had come up in Paris and he had to postpone his trip another week, which was fine by me. At least I had one more week to relax. But now, he was flying in for sure and who the hell knew what category the hurricane was coming in at.

I was sitting in my office when I heard a knock on the door.

"Come in."

"Hey, bro." Danny smiled as he stepped inside."

"Hey. What are you doing here?" I asked as I got up and gave him a light hug.

"Is this a bad time?"

"No. Have a seat. What's up?"

"You know that girl I'm seeing?"

"Lisa, right?"

"Yeah. We were in the car the other day taking a day trip to the country and she said she was dying to listen to this podcast that all her girlfriends were talking about, and she asked if I minded if we listened to it on the drive. I said sure, so she played it."

"And?" I asked.

"And I'm pretty sure it's Jenna."

"What?" I furrowed my brows.

"I'm sending you the link right now," he said as he pulled his phone from his pocket.

I opened up his message on my computer and clicked the link. As I sat there and heard Jenna's voice, I rubbed my face and sighed.

"What is going on with you two?" Danny asked.

"Nothing. We really haven't seen each other all week besides here at the office. She's been going to some prenatal yoga class three times a week and tells me she's busy when I ask her to dinner. I guess she really has been busy. Jesus Christ. I can't believe what I'm hearing."

"There's a total of ten days' worth of podcasts if you want to listen to more. Look at her ratings, bro. She's killing it. I didn't think you knew about it."

"No. I didn't. Thanks for telling me."

I could feel the rage deep inside me. This was the last thing I needed. After Danny left my office, I decided to listen to some clips of a few more. I wouldn't lie. I was offended, and I was pissed as hell.

"Laurel, tell Jenna I want to see her now!"

"Of course, Mr. Thorne."

A few moments later, Jenna walked into my office.

"You wanted to see me?"

"Shut the door and have a seat."

"By the harsh tone of your voice, it sounds serious."

"Oh it is." I pressed play on one of her podcasts.

She sat there and bit down on her bottom lip as we both stared at each other.

"I can explain that."

"You damn well better!" I shouted at her.

"First of all, don't you dare shout at me. Second of all, nobody knows it's you or me."

"Danny fucking knew the minute he heard your voice!" I yelled.

"Why was he listening to my podcast? A little weird, don't you think?"

"His girlfriend was listening to it in the car. It doesn't matter! How could you do that?"

"Do what? Tell my story of being a single pregnant woman whose baby daddy isn't sure if he wants to stick around or not?"

"I told you I would be here for you, but that just wasn't enough. If I didn't want anything to do with you or that baby, I would not have given you a job here or let you rent out my apartment in the same damn building where I was living!"

"Stop shouting."

"No! I won't stop shouting because I'm pissed off! Not to mention the fact that you called me a scared little boy!"

"Hold up." She put her hand up. "I was referring to all men. I wasn't singling you out. But hey, if the shoe fits."

The rage inside me was growing, and I needed to control it before I did something I would regret.

"I need you to leave," I spoke.

"You're done shouting at me?"

"No. But if I continue, I'm afraid I'll say something I'll regret."

"I don't think it's possible for you to regret anything you say or do," she said as she got up from her chair.

"That's where you're wrong. There is something I regret."

Our eyes stayed locked on each other's for what seemed like eternity.

"Point taken, Mr. Thorne."

She left my office, and I slammed my fist down on my desk.

CHAPTER 27

*J*enna

I walked out of his office and Laurel gave me a sympathetic look.

"I'm sorry," she whispered.

"Thanks, but don't be. You know how he is."

Tears filled my eyes as I headed to my office. Grabbing my purse and some personal things I had in my desk, I left the building. Once I made it around the corner, I placed my hands on the side of a building, leaned over and tried to catch my breath as the tears steadily streamed down my face. When I stood up, a severe form of dizziness engulfed me. Everything became blurry and then went dark.

I slowly opened my eyes as I could feel the hard cement under me.

"What—"

"Don't move, miss. An ambulance is on its way," a younger man said as he held something against my forehead.

"What happened?"

"I think you fainted."

"What are you doing?"

I could hear the ambulance in the background.

"You have a pretty bad cut on your forehead. When I called 9-1-1, they told me to keep pressure on it."

The ambulance pulled up and two paramedics were quickly by my side.

"How many weeks pregnant are you?" one of the paramedics asked.

"Almost twenty-six weeks."

"Her blood pressure is really low. We need to get her on fluids immediately," the other paramedic said.

"You have one nasty cut there." The paramedic named Henry smiled as he carefully touched my forehead.

Damn, he was cute.

"Is there anyone I can call for you?" The nice man who was with me when I woke up asked. "Your husband perhaps?"

"No. I don't have a husband or a boyfriend. There's no one to call."

"OH MY GOD, Jenna!" Lindsey exclaimed.

"Ma'am, you need to step back, please," Henry said to her.

"I'm fine, Lindsey."

"What can I do?" she grabbed hold of my hand.

"Ma'am you need to step back."

"Nothing, and don't you dare tell Lucas either. I mean it!"

"Jenna—"

"I mean it!" I voiced loudly as they loaded me into the ambulance.

❧

*L*ucas

I tried to concentrate on work, but I couldn't. Jenna had me so mad and wound up all I could do was sit and stare out the damn window.

"Mr. Thorne?"

"Didn't I tell you that I didn't want to be disturbed?" I shouted at Laurel.

"I know but there's been an accident."

I quickly turned my chair around and stared at her.

"What do you mean? What happened?"

"Lindsey was just on her way to lunch, and she saw an ambulance around the corner. It's Jenna, sir."

"What about, Jenna?" I voiced sternly as I jumped up from my chair and grabbed my suit coat.

"She was lying on the cement and she has a really bad cut on her forehead. The paramedics are taking her to the ER."

"Which one?" I asked in a panic.

"I don't know. I'm sorry."

I ran down the hall and into Lindsey's office.

"What happened to Jenna?"

"All I know is she was lying on the cement and her forehead had a huge gash and it was pouring blood and the paramedic was trying to stop it and the other was giving her fluids," she spoke at a rapid pace.

"Lindsey, BREATHE!" I shouted as I gripped her shoulders. "Which hospital did they take her to?"

"I would assume Mount Sinai. If she asks, I didn't tell you," she shouted as I walked out the door. Stopping, I turned around and looked back at her.

"What do you mean?"

"She made me promise not to tell you. She begged me."

"Of course she did." I shook my head.

~

*J*enna
I laid in the hospital bed and watched my baby's heart rate on the fetal monitor while Matt, the nice man who called 9-1-1 held my hand, and the doctor began to stitch my head.

"You are such a nice person. Thank you for your help."

"You're welcome." He smiled.

Suddenly, standing in the doorway was Lucas. *Shit. Shit. Shit.*

"Oh my God. Are you okay?" he asked. "Excuse me? Who are you, and why are you holding her hand?" he asked Matt in an authoritative tone.

Matt let go and stepped away.

"Apologize to him now!" I demanded. "He was the one who found me and called 9-1-1. He hasn't left my side."

"Jenna, you need to stay still," the doctor said.

"I'm sorry, man." Lucas extended his hand to him. "I didn't know. Thank you for being there for her. I appreciate it."

"You're welcome. And you are who?"

"He's the baby daddy and nothing more."

"Jenna, unless you want a funky looking scar on your head, you have to keep your head still."

"Sorry, doctor."

Matt said his goodbyes and Lucas took hold of my hand. As much as I wanted to jerk it away, I couldn't or else the doctor would have yelled at me.

"What happened?" Lucas asked.

"I don't know."

"Okay. All set," the doctor spoke. "I'll let Dr. Glacier know I'm finished, and he'll be in soon. No stress!" He pointed at me as he looked at both of us.

"I'm going to kill Lindsey," I said.

"She didn't tell me. She kept her promise to you."

"Then how did you find out?"

"She told Laurel, and Laurel told me. And you can't be mad at Lindsey because you told her not to tell me. Which I can't even believe."

"Oh, hello," Dr. Glacier said as he walked in and extended his hand to Lucas. "You are?"

"The baby's father."

"Ah. Okay. Jenna, your blood pressure was dangerously low when the paramedics got to you. All of your other tests came back normal so I don't think there's an underlying condition that would have caused it to drop. Now, being pregnant, and in the trimester you're in right now, it is common for a person's blood pressure to take a dip. But yours took a dive. Have you been under a great deal of stress lately?"

I looked at Lucas and narrowed my eye at him.

"Maybe."

"Alright. Well, stress isn't good for you or the baby. And neither is low blood pressure. The baby's heart rate is good, but you did take a nasty fall and you cut your head open. So, I'm admitting you for the rest of today and overnight just to monitor you and the baby. We want to make sure that your blood pressure stays up, the baby continues to do well, and there's no concussion."

"Okay, Dr. Glacier."

"Once we get you upstairs, we'll do another ultrasound just to be safe. They'll be in to take you up in a few minutes."

"Thank you, doctor," Lucas said.

"You're welcome. By the way, no more stress. Got it?" He pointed at us before walking out of the room.

"Is that the baby's heartbeat I hear?" He smiled as he softly stroked my head.

"Yes." I turned away from him.

"I'm sorry, Jenna. I'm so sorry."

"Don't, Lucas. You can see I'm fine, so go back to the office."

"Nah. You're not getting rid of me that easy. I'm staying here whether you like it or not."

"No. I don't want you to stay out of obligation."

"It's not. I'm staying because I want to be here with you, and I'm not leaving you or our baby's side."

"Your father is flying in tomorrow."

"Actually, he's flying in tonight and he'll be in the office tomorrow. It's probably best I'm not there anyway."

CHAPTER 28

*L*ucas

The feeling I felt when I walked in and saw that man holding Jenna's hand was something I'd never felt before. It was a type of rage that was different than what I usually experienced. My first instinct was to rip him away from her and knock him to the ground. Good thing I didn't. I was grateful to him for helping Jenna and staying with her so she wasn't alone. He was more of a man than I had been.

Seeing Jenna lying in that bed with the cut on her head and hooked up to machines frightened me. The fear of losing her had finally hit me and it rattled me to my core. They took her up to the OB unit so they could monitor her and the baby. The hospital called her OB/GYN doctor, and she was going to come check on Jenna later in the evening.

"Hi, Jenna." A middle-aged woman with long brown hair walked into the room. "I'm Melissa, and I'll be taking care of you for the rest of the afternoon and evening," she spoke as she wrote her name on the whiteboard that hung on the wall. "And you are?" She glanced at me.

"Lucas. I'm the baby's father."

"Nice to meet you, Lucas. I'm going to take your vitals, Jenna. When was the last time you ate?"

"I had breakfast this morning."

"Well, that's not gonna do. We need to get some food in your belly for you and the baby. There's a menu right over there. Find something that sounds good, pick up the phone and place your order. If you want my honest opinion, I'd have this handsome man here go get you something. The food here sucks."

"I can do that," I said.

"Vitals look good, and your blood pressure is almost normal." Melissa smiled. "If you need anything, just push this button right here."

As soon as Melissa walked out, I pulled my phone from my pocket.

"What do you feel like? I can have it here in a flash."

"Thai sounds good."

"Thai it is. There's a Thai place right down the street. What do you want so I can call it in?"

"Pad Thai with chicken. Make sure it's mild. Order a couple spring rolls too."

After I placed the order, I set my phone down and placed my hand on hers.

"They said about fifteen minutes."

"Okay. If you don't mind, I'm just going to close my eyes until the food gets here."

"Not at all." I kissed her forehead.

I sat in the chair and watched her as she closed her eyes, while the steady sounds of our baby's heartbeat galloped in the background. She was almost seven months pregnant and today was the first time I'd heard it. The fact that this was the first time hit me like a ton of bricks. What kind of father was I?

My phone started to buzz and when I picked it up, I saw it was my father calling. Stepping out into the hallway, I answered it.

"Hello, Dad."

"Son. I just landed, and I made reservations for us at Daniel for seven o'clock."

"I'm sorry but I can't tonight. Jenna is in the hospital, and I need to stay with her."

"What happened?"

"She fainted on the street and cut her head. They're keeping her overnight to monitor her and the baby."

"She's in good hands there. You don't need to stay."

I closed my eyes and took in a deep breath.

"I do need to stay, and I am. Whether you like it or not. Dinner will have to wait for another night. And I won't be in the office tomorrow either. I know you can't understand because you don't care about anyone besides yourself. I love her, Dad, and she's my number one priority right not. Not you, not the company, just her and my child. And if you can't grasp that, I'm sorry. You were wrong all these years. For once, I let myself feel and I let myself think, and guess what? Everything is falling into place, not going to hell."

There was a moment of silence on the other end of the phone.

"It seems a lot has changed since our last conversation. We're going to have to discuss that, son."

"Yes, and we will. I have to go."

I ended the call just as I saw the delivery guy walking down the hall with our food.

"Is that order for Thorne?" I asked.

"Yep."

"Thank you." I pulled some cash from my wallet for a tip and handed it to him.

"Thank you, sir. Have a nice night."

"Same to you." I gave him a smile.

I walked into the room and saw Jenna's eyes were open.

"Just in time. The food just got here."

"Did I hear you talking to someone out in the hallway?"

"Just my father. He already landed."

"Is everything okay?"

"Everything is fine." I leaned over and kissed her forehead.

Taking the food from the bag, I set it on her tray and pulled it closer to her while I sat in the chair and we both ate. When we were finished, I had her make me a list of what she needed me to bring her from her apartment.

"I'll be back in a flash." I smiled as I gave her hand a gentle squeeze. "Are you going to be okay while I'm gone?"

"I'll be fine. In fact, I might just sleep for a little bit."

"Good idea. I'll be back soon."

When I arrived at the building, I took the elevator up to her apartment. Sliding the key in the door, I opened it and flipped on the lights. I gasped because nothing had prepared me for what I saw.

CHAPTER 29

*J*enna
I wanted to sleep, but as soon as I'd doze off, a scream woke me up. The screams of a woman in labor. The thought terrified me as it was, and now that I was hearing it from someone else, I was freaked out.

"Here's some more water for you," Melissa said as she set the cup on my tray.

"I take it someone's in labor?"

"Yeah. I'm sorry, honey. Try not to listen or let it bother you. Everyone is different. Your labor might be nothing at all. By the way, that man of yours is very sexy." She grinned.

"He is, but he's not my man. We're just friends who are having a baby."

She narrowed her eye at me. "Okay. Keep telling yourselves that." She smirked. "You should listen to this podcast we've all been listening to. I was the nurse to this patient last week and she was listening to it. It's called—"

"Let me guess. Baby Drama?"

"Yes! You've heard—oh my God. Wait. Jenna Larson. J. Elle. You're J. Elle?!" Her eyes widened.

"Shh." I brought my finger up to my lips.

"Girl. You're like a celebrity around here! And he's the 'friend with benefits?'"

"Yeah." I bit down on my bottom lip.

Suddenly her phone rang and when she looked at it, she had to leave. "We'll talk more about this later." She grinned as she walked out.

I couldn't believe it was taking Lucas so long to get back. I only needed a couple things and I told him exactly where they were. Another thirty minutes had passed, and he finally walked in the room carrying a large glass vase filled with pink and red roses.

"These are for you." He smiled as he set them down.

"They're beautiful. You didn't have to do that."

"I wanted to. The red roses are for you and the pink are for our daughter."

He went to kiss my forehead and I stopped him with my hand and pointed to my lips.

"Are you sure?" he asked.

"I'm positive." I smiled.

He softly brushed his lips against mine.

"Thank you. I love them."

"You're welcome. I'll just set your things over here."

"I was getting worried. What took you so long?"

"There was just a small problem."

"What problem?" I narrowed my eye at him.

"Listen, Jenna. When you get out of here tomorrow, you're going to stay with me in the penthouse."

"Why?"

"Two reasons. The first reason is so I can keep an eye on you, and the second reason is there's a huge hole in the living room ceiling in the apartment and you can't stay there."

"WHAT!" I shouted.

"Calm down." I placed my hands on her shoulders. "Apparently, the hot water tank in the apartment above you broke, and the guy has been out of town the last month, so no one knew. The water has been sitting there for—well, we don't know how long. But it's been long enough to damage the ceiling and create a huge hole and mess." He sighed.

"Oh my God, Lucas. My things."

"Nothing personal of yours was damaged. The couch, the coffee table and the floor took the brunt of it, but who cares about those things. They can be replaced. I'm just thankful that you weren't in the apartment when it happened. I'm taking care of everything, so I don't want you to worry."

"How long until it's livable?" I asked.

"The landlord didn't know, but he said he'll keep me updated."

"I'm so tired. This day has been awful."

"I know and I'm sorry." He leaned over and brushed his lips against mine.

"Good evening, you two." Dr. Lewis smiled as she walked into the room.

"Hi, Dr. Lewis. This is Lucas Thorne, the baby's father."

"Nice to meet you, Mr. Thorne."

"Likewise, Dr. Lewis."

"How are you feeling, Jenna?"

"I'm feeling much better."

"Your blood pressure is up and looking good and the baby's heart rate is perfect. I know they did an ultrasound down in the emergency room, but I want to do one more just to be safe."

I looked at Lucas and he gave me a warm smile as he held my hand. Dr. Lewis pulled up my gown, squirted some gel on my belly and moved the transducer back and forth over it.

"You weren't here for the last ultrasound, were you?" she asked Lucas.

"No. I wasn't. I was out of town."

"Well, here's your daughter." Dr. Lewis smiled.

"Wow. She looks so much bigger than her last picture," he said.

"That's because she's grown since then."

I looked at Lucas, and the smile on his face as he stared at the monitor melted my heart.

"Everything looks great. Your daughter is thriving. Just get some rest tonight and you can go home tomorrow after breakfast. I want you to take it easy and rest the next three days, and I want to see you in my office next week for a recheck on your blood pressure. We're going to have to monitor that very closely now until the baby is born. But more importantly, I want you to stay hydrated and stress free."

"I will, Dr. Lewis. Thank you."

"You're welcome. It was nice to meet you, Mr. Thorne. Take care."

"You look tired," I said to Lucas. "You should go home and get some rest."

"I'm not going anywhere. I'm staying with you tonight."

"No, Lucas. You need to sleep in your own bed."

"No, Jenna. I need to be where you are. I won't sleep a wink at home knowing you're in here by yourself. Scoot over and let me climb in with you until you fall asleep."

I gave him a wide smile as I moved over as much as I could. He climbed in and pulled me close as he rested his hand on my belly.

CHAPTER 30

*L*ucas
    I lay there with her and for the first time in my life, every-thing felt right. She told me earlier that she doubted I would ever regret anything I said or did. My biggest regret was not telling her how I truly felt. It took almost losing her to finally admit that I loved her. I hated myself for that. I'd made a promise to her when I got back from Maine that I'd always be here for her, and I was. Just not in the way she needed me to be. As my hand rested on her belly, I felt the baby kick. Glancing over at Jenna, she was sound asleep. I slowly moved my hand across her belly, and with each movement, came another kick. I didn't want to leave the bed, but she needed to be comfortable, and the bed just wasn't big enough for two people. Instead of sleeping on the pull-out couch in the room, I brought the lounge chair up to the bed and held her hand while I slept.

~

I opened my eyes and smiled when I saw Jenna was awake and staring at me.

"Good morning," I spoke.

"Good morning." A bright smile crossed her face. "Why did you sleep in that uncomfortable chair?"

"The couch is too far, and I wanted to be closer to you in case you needed something. Plus, this chair isn't that bad," I said as I struggled to get up.

She let out a soft laugh.

"Okay. Maybe it isn't so comfortable after all. How are you feeling?" I asked as I leaned over and kissed her forehead.

"I'm ready to go home."

"I know, and you will soon. I'll go get us some coffee. Do you want anything else?"

"To go home." She smiled.

I let out a laugh as I walked out of the room and headed down to the coffee bar. When I got back to the room, Jenna had already changed into the new clothes I'd brought her.

"Planning on leaving so soon?" I smirked as I handed the coffee cup to her.

"I just want to be ready for when they discharge me."

A couple hours later, we walked into the building and she wanted to stop at her apartment first to grab a few things. As I unlocked the door and she stepped inside, she stood and stared at the disaster in the living room.

"Wow. This really sucks," she spoke as she stared up at the large hole in the ceiling.

"I don't think it does." I smiled.

"What?" She cocked her head at me. "How can you not think this totally sucks?"

"Because now you get to live with me." I kissed the side of her head.

My phone rang, and when I pulled it from my pocket, I saw my father was calling, so I hit decline. I'd deal with him later. After helping her pack her suitcase, I took her up to the penthouse and placed her suitcase in my bedroom.

"I'm going to take a shower and then when I get out, we need to talk," I said as I brushed my lips against hers.

"I know we do." The corners of her mouth curved upward as her hands were planted on my chest. "But I think you should go to work for a while first."

"Not today." I stroked her cheek.

"What about your father?"

"What about him? He can wait until I come back. Until then, you're my priority. Now go lay down and rest. I won't be long."

~

*J*enna

While Lucas was in the shower, I went to the kitchen and made a cup of coffee. As I held the cup in my hand, I walked over to the large windows in the living room and stared out at the beautiful city view.

"I thought I told you to lay down and rest."

"You do realize you can't tell me what to do, right?" I grinned.

"I know." He let out a sigh. "I've noticed that if I tell you to do something, you do the opposite."

"It's still the inner kid in me rebelling."

He walked over to the window, grabbed my hand and led me to the couch.

"I have a lot to say to you. Things I'm not used to saying to anyone. So, if I screw this up, I need you to promise me you'll forgive me."

"I can do that." I grinned.

"The first thing I want to do is apologize to you. I'm sorry for everything I said and did that hurt you. You might think I said and did those things on purpose to hurt you, but I didn't. I did it to protect myself from the reeling emotions that were inside me from the first moment I saw you. You know how my father always said, 'If you feel, you stop thinking, and when you stop thinking everything goes to hell.'"

"How could I forget such stupidity."

I let out a chuckle.

"When I was twenty-two, I met this girl and fell head over heels for her instantly. She occupied my mind day and night, and I would have done anything for her. I kept her a secret from my father because I knew he wouldn't be happy, and I couldn't let him jeopardize our relationship. Then one day, I screwed up a multi-million-dollar deal. A screw up so big that we lost the contract. And the only reason I screwed it up was because I had just found out that she was cheating on me with a friend of mine. My father knew something was up and he badgered me until I finally told him. Instead of saying he was sorry and trying to comfort me, he lectured me, screamed at me, warned me, and threatened me. He pounded into my head that it was the feelings I had for her that distracted me and cost him millions of dollars. After you're told something for so long, you believe it. So, I never let myself get emotionally involved with another woman after that. But then I met you." He smiled. "After our first night together, I knew if I kept seeing you, I'd fall down that rabbit hole of emotions, and I couldn't let that happen."

"Then I told you I was pregnant," I said.

"Yes, and then I really freaked out. And the more time we spent together, the harder my feelings for you hit me. But I was too scared to admit it. That's why our friendship worked for a while. Because I could have you in my life without having to admit that I loved you. But I failed you, Jenna, and for that I'm sorry. I was so selfish with my own fears and needs, I completely dismissed yours. Then when Laurel walked into my office and told me what happened yesterday, I had never felt so scared in my life. The thought of losing you and our daughter terrified me, and I won't ever let that happen again. I'm not my father, nor will I ever be. And I refuse to live the miserable life he does." He brought his hand up to my cheek. "I love you, Jenna Larson. I have loved you, I am in love with you, and I plan on loving you for the rest of my life. If you'll let me because I know how stubborn and defiant you can be." The corners of his mouth curved upward. "But that's what I love about you."

"Are you done?" I asked as tears sprung to my eyes.

"I think so."

"I love you too, Lucas. As much as I tried to fight it, I couldn't. And even when you were a total asshole, I couldn't stop, because I knew deep down inside you were an amazing man. You truly are an amazing man, and you're going to be an amazing father. I love you so much that sometimes it really hurts."

"I know the feeling, baby." He stroked my cheek.

When I heard that, I scrunched up my face.

"Don't call me that."

"Yeah. I'm not sure why I even said it to be honest."

"Babe is fine," I said.

"'Babe'. I like it."

"I can call you that too, if you don't mind."

"I don't mind at all. I think I'd actually enjoy it." The corners of his mouth curved upward.

"Okay, babe. You got it." I smiled as I brushed my lips against his. "I'm sorry about the podcast."

"Don't you dare be sorry for that. I'm the one who is sorry for the way I reacted. It's just when I heard it, it hurt. I knew I failed you, and I hated myself for it. You are killing it in the podcast world, and you keep doing what you're doing. Especially if you're helping other women."

"Thank you. I love you."

"I love you more, babe." He grinned. "You do know that you're living here permanently, right?"

"I am?" I cocked my head at him with a smile.

"Yes. Because I want my girl—girl—girl—"

"G.I.R.L.F.R.I.E.N.D," I slowly said the word.

"Yes. My girlfriend and my daughter with me twenty-four hours a day, seven days a week. I want to wake up to you every morning, have every meal with you, and I want to hold you and kiss you goodnight every single night. I want you to stick around forever, Jenna."

"I already planned on it." I grinned.

"Is that so?" His brow arched.

"Yes. Because up here on the 82nd floor, you don't have to worry about apartment ceilings above you caving in."

"Ah. I see. But up here on the 82nd floor, there is a slight possibility of the roof caving in. Just a slight one though."

"Oh. I didn't think about that." I bit down on my bottom lip.

"I wouldn't worry about it too much." He kissed my forehead.

CHAPTER 31

*L*ucas

Opening my eyes, I lay there and watch Jenna as she peacefully slept. Having her in my bed and knowing she was permanently a part of it, made me feel incredibly good. The only problem I had now was my father, and I wasn't sure what was going to happen. But I had a plan. A plan that involved me leaving Thorne Tech and starting my own company. I had my own family now, and I needed to get out from the grips of my father.

As much as I wanted to stay in bed with her all day, I needed to shower and get to the office to face the wrath of my father. When I finished showering, I stepped out and wrapped a towel around my waist. Walking into the bedroom, I saw Jenna staring at me with a smile on her face.

"Good morning." I grinned as I walked over and kissed her.

"Good morning. I woke up and you weren't here."

"Sorry, babe. I had to get in the shower, and I didn't want to wake you." I took a seat on the edge of the bed.

"Are you nervous about seeing your father?" she asked as she stroked my arm.

"Nah. I'm fully prepared to clean out my office today and never look back."

"I'm sorry you're going through this."

"Don't be." I smiled as I brought my thumb up to her chin. "We're starting a new chapter in our lives and my father will not be a part of it. Besides, I look forward to starting my own company and building it from the ground up. Now I have to finish getting ready." I gave her another kiss.

After I finished getting dressed, I went down to the kitchen and said goodbye to Jenna.

"I have to go. I love you." I brushed my lips against hers.

"I love you too. Good luck."

"Thanks." I gave her a wink. Bending down, I pressed my lips against her belly. "Have a good day, princess."

~

I set my briefcase down in my office, took in a deep breath and headed to see my father. Opening the door, I stepped inside.

"Well, look what the cat dragged in. Sit down," he spoke in an authoritative voice.

"Actually, Dad, before you go off on me and tell me what a rotten selfish son I am, I have a few words to say to you."

"Go ahead. I'm listening."

"I love Jenna and I love the fact that we're having a child together. I've asked her to move in with me and she agreed. When the time is right, I'm going to ask her to marry me, and if you have a problem with it, that's too fucking bad. I've lived my entire life trying to please you and I'm done. I'm living my own life now on my terms and my terms only. If you want to fire me, go ahead. I don't care. Jenna and my daughter are more important to me, and I would give everything up for them."

"For God sakes, are you finished?" His brow arched.

"Yes. I'm finished."

"Sit the hell down." He pointed to the chair across from his desk. "I'm not firing you. You're a part of this company and you're my only son. The way you stood up to me the other day over the phone made me proud."

"It did?" I cocked my head in disbelief.

"It did, son. You've never stood up to me before, and I got to thinking about a lot of things after our phone call. The drama show you just put on was a little uncalled for, but again, it made me proud. You're standing up for something you believe in and you're fighting for it. That's what makes you a man. I've decided that I'm retiring next year, and I'm giving you fifty-one percent ownership of Thorne Technology. The entire company will be yours, son.

"Why are you retiring?"

"Because I'm tired of the business and I know I don't need to worry about anything as long as you're sitting in my chair and that little genius girlfriend of yours is by your side. I'm going to dissolve the Paris division, so you won't need to worry about that."

"What are you going to do with all your free time?" I asked.

"Travel the world and see everything I've always wanted before my time expires."

"Sounds like a good plan, Dad."

"I'm looking forward to it. Now go on and get out of here. I'm sure you have a shitload of work to do." He smiled.

"I do. Thanks, Dad."

"Get out of here, son. And by the way, I'm happy Jenna and the baby are okay."

I walked out of his office in disbelief but on cloud-nine. When I got back to my office, I immediately called Jenna.

"Hello."

"Hey, babe."

"How did it go?"

"I would rather tell you in person. Lunch today?"

"Definitely. Meet me at Central Park on Cherry Hill at twelve-thirty and we can have a picnic. We don't have very many warm days left."

"Sounds wonderful. I'll see you then. I love you."

"I love you too, babe."

~

I could see her lying on a blanket in her long dress looking up at the sky. It was the most beautiful sight I'd ever seen. She turned her head and smiled at me as I approached her. Bending down, I gave her belly a kiss before moving up to her lips.

"Hi." I smiled.

"Hi."

"These are for you," I spoke as I handed her a mixed bouquet of beautiful flowers.

"They're beautiful. Thank you." She grinned as I took her hand and helped her sit up.

I took a seat on the blanket next to her while she opened the white picnic basket and took out a couple sandwiches and fresh fruit.

"So, how did it go? Did you quit?"

"I didn't have to."

"Oh no. He fired you?"

"No." I let out a laugh. "He's retiring next year and giving me fifty-one percent ownership of the company."

"What?"

"I know. I'm shocked too. He's going to travel the world when he retires. He said he was proud of me for the way I stood up to him."

"Wow. What happened to him?"

"I don't know, and I don't care. I'm not questioning any of it."

"That is wonderful news, babe." She grinned as she wrapped her arms around my neck and hugged me.

"He said he didn't need to worry about the company as long as I was sitting in his chair and had you by my side."

"He's a smart man." She smiled as she broke our embrace.

"That he is." I kissed her.

CHAPTER 32

ONE MONTH LATER

*J*enna

    I stood in the bathroom mirror as tears fell down my face.

"What's wrong?" Lucas asked as he stepped out of the shower.

"My boobs are leaking." I pointed to the round wet spots on my nightshirt. "I'm fat as fuck, my back hurts, I have hemorrhoids, I can barely put my shoes on, and I have to pee every five minutes while you stand there looking as perfect and sexy as ever with your defined six pack and stupid god like body. I hate you." I walked out of the bathroom.

I heard him chuckle as he walked over and wrapped his arms around me from behind.

"You are incredibly perfect and beautiful just as you are, and I love you so much."

"You're just saying that to make me feel better."

"Do you feel that?" he asked as he pushed his body against me. "This is how much you turn me on, leaky boobs, hemorrhoids, and all." He pressed his lips against the side of my neck, and I couldn't help but smile. "As much as I want to show you how sexy you are, you better get dressed because the guys will be here shortly to finish the nursery and the furniture is being delivered today. Now stop being silly. I love you, babe."

"I love you too." I turned around in his arms and pressed my lips against his.

~

*L*ucas

I waited at the elevator because the workers were on their way up.

"Morning, Mr. Thorne," Jimmy and Wes spoke at the same time.

"Good morning. Listen, I need you to do me a favor."

"Sure. What do you need?"

"I need you to give Jenna a few compliments. She's feeling really bad about herself right now." I gave them each a fifty-dollar bill.

"Thank you, Mr. Thorne, but you don't need to pay us to give her compliments. We give them out for free."

"Just take it and buy yourself something with it. You guys have done a great job in the nursery."

"Well, in that case, thank you again."

I patted Jimmy on the back, and they headed up to the nursery.

When I walked into the kitchen, I saw Jenna leaning against the island holding a cup of coffee and scrolling on her phone.

"Was that Jimmy and Wes?" she asked.

"Yeah. They should only be here a couple hours. I got a text message from the delivery guys and they'll be here around three o'clock."

"Okay. I made a cup of coffee for Jimmy and Wes. Grab one and follow me to the nursery. Good morning boys," Jenna said as we handed them a cup of coffee.

"Good morning. You look absolutely beautiful today, Miss Larson," Jimmy spoke.

"Yeah. You're like glowing." Wes smiled.

"You're one of the prettiest pregnant women I've ever seen." Jimmy grinned.

"Thank you. You're very kind and I appreciate your compliments. If you need anything, you know where to find me."

"You're welcome. You look stunning," Wes said as we walked out of the room.

"How much did you pay them to throw compliments my way?" she asked, and I knew I was in deep shit.

"I have no idea what you're talking about, babe."

"It was a little over the top, don't you think?" A smirk crossed her lips.

"I thought it was very nice of them to say what they did."

She rolled her eyes at me and went into her office to record a podcast.

I went down to the apartment on the fiftieth floor to inspect the final repairs of the ceiling. Everything looked great so I called my realtor and had her put it up for sale. There was no use in keeping the apartment any longer, not even for investments reasons. I had another investment I was working on as a surprise for Jenna.

~

One Month Later

*J*enna

I sat in the rocking chair in the nursery and held the gray stuffed elephant Lucas had bought against my belly. As I slowly rocked back and forth, I had a little chat with my daughter.

"Listen up, kid. We have two weeks left until you make your arrival into the world. Mommy would be so grateful if you could speed it up a bit. Not today or anything, maybe just by a week. And whatever you do, do not be late. Because honestly, my back can't take anymore. I'm just so excited to meet you and hold you in my arms. So, feel free to come out anytime in the next week."

"Are you telling our daughter to hurry up and be born?" Lucas smiled as he stood in the doorway with his arms folded.

"Basically." I smiled.

He walked over to me, took my hand, helped me up from the chair, and we started dancing.

"I can't wait to meet her." He smiled as we swayed back and forth.

Suddenly, I felt a trickling sensation running down my legs. I let go of his hand and looked down.

"Did you just pee on the floor or did your water just break?" he asked in a panic.

"I don't know." I looked up at him. "How do we tell?"

"I have no clue. Shouldn't you know these things?"

"Have I ever been pregnant before?" I asked with irritation in my voice.

"Well, go sit on the toilet and I'll get the book. It has to say something about that."

"Good idea."

I sat down on the toilet and Lucas walked in with the book.

"It says if it only happens once then it's probably urine or vaginal discharge. It also says to wait a few hours and see. I bet you just peed. Nothing to worry about. Right?"

"You're right. She is pressing really hard on my bladder. Can you help me up?"

"Of course, babe." He held out his hand and the moment I stood up, a gush of fluid hit the bathroom floor.

We both looked down and then up at each other.

"I don't think that's pee," Lucas said.

"I don't either. I think my water broke." I sighed.

"I'll grab your bag and call Thaddeus to meet us downstairs."

"OH MY FREAKING GOD!" I yelled as I doubled over in sudden pain.

"Are you okay?" Lucas came running into the bathroom.

"DO I LOOK OKAY?" I shouted.

"Shit. Come on, babe. We really have to go."

He grabbed my bag and hooked his arm around me as we slowly walked to the elevator.

"Oh my God, Lucas."

"It's okay, babe. Just get in the elevator and we'll get you to the hospital."

I was highly agitated. Not just from the pain, but from the way the damn elevator kept stopping on different floors.

I grabbed his shirt.

"I just want you to know that I hate you for living on the 82nd floor. Hate you!"

"Duly noted, babe."

When the elevator finally stopped on the floor of the lobby, I had to stop for a second while another contraction hit.

"OH MY GOD!" I doubled over in pain.

"Not need to panic. She's in labor." Lucas smiled at the people who were staring.

"Do you need help, Mr. Thorne?" Russell came running over.

"Thaddeus is waiting outside for us. We need to get Jenna to the hospital."

"Okay. It stopped. I can make it to the car," I spoke.

We were on our way to the hospital and the contractions were coming four minutes apart. I could barely breathe I was in so much pain.

"Are we almost there because I feel like this baby is coming right now!" I shouted.

"Jenna, you are not having our baby in the back our car. Hold her in."

"Oh okay, Lucas. You idiot." I slapped his chest.

"Listen, don't get an attitude with me. You're the one who just told her it was okay to come now."

"You'd be wise not to say another word to me!" I shouted.

The car pulled up to the entrance of the ER, and Thaddeus ran inside to alert someone while Lucas tried to help me out of the car and into the wheelchair a nurse had brought out.

"I'm going to take you up to Labor and Delivery," she spoke as she wheeled me inside.

"Listen to me, lady. I won't make it. This baby is coming NOW!" I shouted.

"Okay." She pushed the button on the wall while I let out a couple more screams. "What's going on here? Why aren't you taking her up to Labor and Delivery?" a doctor asked as he walked over.

"She said the baby is coming right now."

"Is this your first baby?" he asked me.

"Yes."

"Of course. First time moms." He sighed.

"What did you say!" I shouted and Lucas gripped my shoulder.

"Get her in room four and in a gown so I can take a look. Call me when she's ready."

"I feel the need to kill him, Lucas."

"No you don't, babe. It's the pain talking. Just try to breathe through it," he said as he and the nurse helped me change into a gown.

"I need this kid out of me right now, Lucas. Just go down there and get her out. Please." I begged.

"I'm going to check you, Jenna. Okay?" the nice nurse said. "Oh boy. You are having this baby now." She ran out of the room.

Another contraction hit and I had to push. I couldn't help it as I let out a scream.

"Breathe. Breathe through it," Lucas spoke.

"Tell me to breathe again and I swear to God I'll scratch your eyes out."

The doctor and nurse came running in. He pulled up a stool and sat down.

"You weren't kidding. Your baby is coming."

"NO SHIT!" I yelled. "NOW APOLOGIZE!"

"Get the fetal monitor hooked up," he said to the nurse. "I've called Dr. Lewis and she's here at the hospital. She's on her way down now."

"Thank God. Oh God, here comes another one."

"Push, Jenna. One big push!"

I pushed with everything I had as Lucas supported my back and tightly held my hand.

"I see her head, babe. She's coming."

I fell back on the bed and I wanted to die. I felt like I was being ripped in half.

156

"Hello, Jenna. Oh look at that, I see a head." She smiled. "I can take over from here. All I need from you is one more push. The biggest push you got and then it will all be over. Okay?"

I nodded my head as Lucas helped me up and I let out a scream as I pushed my daughter out. Instantly, I felt relief when I heard her cry.

"And here she is. Two weeks early. I guess she couldn't wait to meet her mom and dad."

Tears of joy fell down my face as Dr. Lewis laid her on my belly.

"You did it, babe. She's beautiful. Look at how beautiful she is." Lucas cried as he kissed my cheek.

"Hey there, Scarlett Elyse Thorne." I reached out and touched her tiny hand.

CHAPTER 33

TWO WEEKS LATER

*L*ucas

Life with a newborn. What could I say? It had been a tough past couple of weeks. We were sleep deprived and Scarlett was feeding every hour and refusing to sleep. Jenna started pumping into bottles so I could relieve her every now and again. Especially in the middle of the night so she could get some rest.

I had worked from home the past couple weeks so I could be here for Jenna and the baby. But now it was time for me to get back into the office. I tried to hire a baby nurse to help her out while I was gone, but Jenna wouldn't hear of it. I kept the number close by just in case she changed her mind.

"I have to go now, babe. I'm sorry." I kissed her lips as she stood in the kitchen holding Scarlett.

"Don't be sorry. We'll be fine."

"I'm going to miss you girls so much."

"Babe, I know you're secretly excited about getting out. You can't fool me."

"How dare you say that. That is not true." I kissed her forehead and then kissed Scarlett goodbye.

Once I hit the doors to the outside, I let out a sigh of relief. I loved them both so much and they consumed me. But fuck yeah, I was looking forward to going to the office.

~

*J*enna

I'd finally got Scarlett down for a nap and sat behind my desk to record a podcast about the first two weeks of parenthood. As I was talking, I started to cry. I wasn't sure why except I knew I was exhausted, both mentally and physically. Instead of stopping the recording, I cried my way through it for I promised my listeners I would be open and raw about my experiences. Just as I finished recording, I decided to lay down and try to take a nap. Grabbing the baby monitor, I quietly entered our bedroom. Peeking into the bassinet that sat next to the bed, she looked like a peaceful little angel. So I carefully laid down on the bed and smiled when my head hit the pillow. My eyes weren't closed for a minute before the ear-piercing cries started.

"No. No. No," I whispered as I reached over and gripped the edge of the bassinet and slowly rocked it back and forth which only made her scream more.

Picking her up from the bassinet, I unbuttoned my shirt and fed her for the hundredth time today. When she was finished, I changed her diaper, took her downstairs and set her in her swing. Immediately she started to scream and the moment I picked her up and held her, she stopped. An hour later, she finally fell asleep, and I desperately needed some coffee, so I set her in her swing, turned it on and headed to the kitchen. My coffee had just finished brewing when I heard the elevator ding. As I ran to the foyer, Lucas had just stepped out, and I immediately placed my hand over his mouth before he could say anything.

"Wake her up and die," I whispered.

He nodded his head, so I removed my hand. He gave me a tender kiss and then pointed in the direction of the bedroom. After I grabbed my coffee from the kitchen, I walked to the bedroom, shut the door and talked to him as he changed out of his suit.

"You didn't shower today?" he asked.

"Excuse me? What did you say?"

"I said, you can take a shower now that I'm home."

"That's what I thought you said."

"Come here." He held his arms out to me and I immediately fell into them.

"How was work?" I asked.

"It was okay. I missed the two of you terribly."

"We missed you too, babe."

"So, what about dinner? Did you—"

"What about dinner? And did I what?" I cocked my head at him.

"Did you decide what you're in the mood for? Your choice. Anything you want."

"Pizza?"

"Excellent choice. I'll call it in right now."

After Lucas called in the pizza, we walked to the living room, and I saw the wide grin on his face when he saw Scarlett was awake.

"Your daddy's home, princess," he spoke to her as he took her from the swing and sat down on the couch. "Daddy missed his sweet girl so much," he said as kept kissing her cheeks.

Watching him with her melted me in every way possible. Especially when I thought back to a time not so long ago when he told me he couldn't be a father. Every time I saw him with her and that thought popped in my head, I would start to tear up.

We had just finished dinner when Scarlett started to cry.

"Do you think she's hungry?" Lucas asked as he held her.

"Probably. When isn't she hungry?"

"Here. You better take her then."

"Oh no. I'm going to take a hot relaxing bath. You can grab a bottle from the refrigerator and feed her since you haven't seen her all day." I placed my hand on his chest and smiled.

"Yes. Of course. Go take your bath, babe." He kissed my forehead.

I went to the bathroom and locked the door. After pouring some lavender scented bubbles under the stream of hot water, I climbed in and let out a sigh of relief as I took in the silence around me. Closing my eyes, I took myself to a place filled with peace and released all the tension in my body. I was fully relaxed until I heard him walk into the bedroom with a screaming baby and jiggled the doorknob to the bathroom.

"Hey, babe?"

"What?"

"She won't stop crying. I don't know what to do for her."

"Did you burp her?"

"Yes."

"Did you change her diaper?"

"Yes."

"Then I don't know what to tell you. Figure it out! But whatever you do, don't let her fall asleep or she'll be up the entire night."

"Okay. I won't."

I closed my eyes again and took in the silence.

"Hey, babe. You've been in there for over an hour."

"What's your point, Lucas?" I shouted.

"I miss you."

"I'll be out in a minute." I rolled my eyes.

After drying off and slipping into my robe, I opened the door and saw Lucas sitting on the bed on his laptop.

"Did you enjoy your bath?" He smiled and closed his laptop.

"Very much."

I climbed on the bed and right into his arms. He felt so good, and I wanted to stay like this forever.

"Lucas?"

"Yeah, babe?"

"Where's the baby?"

"I put her down in her crib for now so we can spend some time alone, and I put on the star projector for her. That should keep her quiet for a few minutes. I have a surprise for you."

"If it isn't at least twelve hours of uninterrupted sleep, I don't want it."

He let out a chuckle and reached into the drawer of his nightstand.

"I think you'll enjoy this." He held an envelope in front of my face as my head laid on his chest.

Taking the envelope from him, I sat up and opened it.

"A day at the spa for this Saturday?"

"Yep. Saturday is your day to be pampered."

"And you're going to be home with Scarlett all day, alone?" I arched my brow.

"Of course. She's my daughter. We're going to have a lot of daddy/daughter time."

"You are the best baby daddy ever, and I love you so much." I leaned over and kissed his lips.

~

Spa Day

"Are you sure you're going to be okay?" I asked Lucas as I put my shoes on.

"We're going to be just fine. Go enjoy your day and don't worry about us. Today is all about you relaxing." He kissed my forehead.

"I don't know what time I'll be home."

"You take as long as you want. We're going to have so much fun today, aren't we, princess?" Lucas spoke to her as he held her in his arms.

After giving him a kiss on the lips, I gave Scarlett a kiss and stepped into the elevator. The moment I stepped outside the building, I threw my hands up in the air. Freedom was mine for a day, and I was going to enjoy every minute of it. But as I was on my way to the spa, I felt this tremendous feeling of guilt wash over me. I shouldn't be doing this. I need to be home with my baby. I was gone ten minutes and I already missed her terribly. This wasn't a good idea and I needed to go back home.

"Thaddeus, turn around and take me back to the penthouse."

"I'm sorry, Jenna, but I can't do that."

"What? What do you mean?"

"Lucas knew you'd probably say that, and he gave me strict instructions not to listen to you."

"Oh come on. I need to go home."

"You need this day more. It's important you take care of yourself, Jenna. Consider it a mental health day and a chance to regroup so you can continue being the amazing mother you are."

"Thanks, Thaddeus." I smiled.

A two-hour body massage, some reflexology, facial, manicure, pedicure and an invigorating essential oil steam treatment made up my day. I felt renewed, relaxed and for the first time in two weeks, my mind was clear.

"Well?" Thaddeus smiled as he opened the car door for me.

"Best day ever, Thaddeus." I grinned.

When I stepped off the elevator, all was quiet. Too quiet in fact. Setting my purse down, I walked into the kitchen and it was a disaster. Bottles and dishes were everywhere. Walking to the bedroom, I smiled when I saw Lucas asleep with Scarlett sleeping on his chest. I softly kissed his forehead and his eyes opened.

"Wake her up and die," he whispered.

CHAPTER 34

TWO MONTHS LATER

*L*ucas

It was hard to believe Scarlett was already three months old. She was growing and changing so quickly. The first month was the hardest. Hell, it was still hard. I wouldn't lie. My daughter was a very alert child who didn't seem to need much sleep. But Jenna developed a routine and made sure we both stuck to it. Things were a little easier now that Scarlett was sleeping at least five hours during the night. We never thought the day would come, but it did, and we took what we could get.

While Jenna was asleep with her head on my chest, I reached over and pulled the ring out I had hidden in the nightstand. After I slipped it on her finger, she stirred. My heart was racing a mile a minute and I was nervous as hell. When she opened her eyes, the first thing she noticed was the large diamond ring on her finger. She looked up at me and the shocked expression on her face made me smile.

"Will you marry me, babe?"

"Oh my God." A wide grin crossed her lips as she sat up and stared into my eyes. "Yes! Oh my God, Lucas. I would love to marry you."

Wrapping my arms around her, I rolled her on her back and hovered over her.

"You have made me the happiest man in the world, and I love you so much." I kissed her. "I was going to wait and do it the proper way down on one knee. But then I figured once I got down on my knee, you'd know what I was doing, and I wanted you to be totally surprised."

"You did it perfectly, and I can't wait to marry you and call you my husband."

Suddenly, we heard Scarlett's cries through the monitor.

"Let's go tell our daughter the good news." I grinned as I kissed Jenna's lips.

While Jenna was feeding the baby, I took a shower and got ready for work.

"By the way, I have to go to Maine for some business for a few days and I want you and Scarlett to come with me," I said as I put on my tie.

"That sounds fun. We'd love to go with you. When are we leaving?"

"Tomorrow morning."

"Oh. Thanks for the notice, Thorne."

I turned to her and gave her a smile.

"Sorry, babe. It was kind of a last-minute thing."

"No worries. I'll just add packing to the list of things I have to do today. Can you take her for me? I need to pee."

"Of course. Come here, princess. Let Daddy hold you before he leaves for the day."

She smiled at me and began to coo as I held her. "You are the most beautiful baby in the entire world and I already know I'm going to have problems when the boys start coming around." I held her up and she vomited all over my designer suit.

"Hey, babe?" I shouted. "Can you add taking my suit to the cleaners to your list? Scarlett just threw up all over me.

"Were you moving her too much? You know she just ate."

"Uh, maybe."

"Then you can take your suit in yourself. You know better than that, babe. We've talked about this before." She smirked as she walked out of the bathroom.

165

~

*J*enna

We landed in Portland, Maine, and climbed into the SUV Lucas had rented.

"Which hotel are we staying at?" I asked.

"We're not. I got us an Airbnb instead."

"Ah. Good idea." I smiled as I reached over and stroked his cheek. "How far is this Airbnb?"

"We'll be there in about forty-five minutes." He smiled as he glanced over at me.

The drive to the Airbnb was beautiful as I took in the winding roads and snowcapped trees. Lucas made a right hand turn on a dirt road that led to a secluded home. Beautiful tall trees, trails and a lake made up the surrounding area.

"Wow. This looks great." I smiled as I climbed out of the car and stared at the house.

Lucas grabbed the car seat while I grabbed a couple of our bags.

"Babe, leave those. I'll come back for them."

"I got it." I smiled as we walked up to the door.

Stepping inside, a peaceful feeling washed over me.

"This is so nice. How did you find this place?"

"Come with me. I want to show you something," he said as he set the car seat down.

He took my hand and led me to the back of the house and opened the sliding door.

"Look at that view, babe."

"It's gorgeous," I said as I stepped on to the deck. "Wow. It's so peaceful here."

"I know. This is where I stayed when I came here for a couple weeks."

"Here? This exact house?"

"Yep, and I never once stopped thinking about it."

I looked over at him as he stared out into the lake.

"I bought the house, Jenna. I bought it for our family." He hooked his arm around me and pulled me into him. "And I'm praying you love it just as much as I do."

"This is our house?"

"Our house, babe. I thought we could spend a lot of time here in the summer and fall months. This lake house will become part of the Thorne legacy for generations to come."

"I love it, Lucas. I truly love it."

"Come inside. There's something else I want to show you."

He pulled out what looked like drawings and unrolled it across the kitchen table.

"What's this?"

"The plans for the house I had drawn up. It's only a two-bedroom, one bath, which isn't big enough for us. We are definitely going to need more room. Especially when our family starts growing." He smiled as he gave me a wink. "I bought the land next door and I want to expand the house. We'll make the kitchen bigger and add a few more bathrooms and bedrooms. What do you think?"

"I love it." I reached up and kissed his cheek.

"Are you sure? I want you to really look at these drawings and tell me what you want or don't want. Because you're going to be involved every step of the way."

"We're not here on business, are we?" I smiled.

"No. I used that as an excuse to get you here and surprise you."

"You are just full of surprises lately. Was the house up for sale?"

"No." He chuckled. "I made the owners an offer they absolutely couldn't turn down. In fact, they didn't even hesitate when I made the offer in cash."

"I can't believe you did this for us. I love you so much, and we're going to be so happy here."

"I love you too, babe, and all I want is to spend the rest of my life with you."

"You've got me for life, Lucas." I grinned as our lips met. "How long is the house going to take?"

"The contractor said three months tops because this is the only project they'll be working on. I made sure of that. And the timing will be perfect because the warmer weather will be settling in and we can be here in the summer."

CHAPTER 35

THREE MONTHS LATER

*J*enna

"Okay. Let's do this." I turned and looked at Lucas as I grabbed his hand.

We walked over to Scarlett who was sitting up on her playmat. She started sitting up on her own over a month ago and started crawling less than two weeks ago. I started piecing her milestones together and I became very nervous. When I called my mother and told her everything Scarlett was doing, she said I did the same things at her age.

We both sat down across from her and Lucas placed the wooden block set in front of her. We spread out the different shapes around her and let her go at it. She picked up the round block first and brought it up to her mouth. Then she tried to place it in the square hole. Her coordination skills were a little advanced for her age.

"Look at her Lucas, she's analyzing."

"Come on, Jenna. No she isn't."

"No. Look at her. She's staring at the round hole."

Suddenly, she moved the block over to the round hole and dropped it in. Lucas and I looked at each other.

"What a smart girl." Lucas smiled as he handed her the square block. "Show Mommy and Daddy where this one goes."

Without hesitating, she put it in the square hole.

"I told you she was analyzing!" I hit his arm. "Oh my God, she takes after me." Tears started to fill my eyes.

"Are those tears of happiness?"

"I don't know. I'm scared for her."

"There's no reason to be. We pretty much knew that between my brain and yours she was going to be somewhat intelligent."

"This goes beyond somewhat intelligent, Lucas."

"And we'll deal with it step by step and day by day. Who knows, she may grow up and do something that could change the world." He hooked his arm around me and pulled me into him.

~

Six Months Later

"I present to you Mr. and Mrs. Lucas Thorne."

Everyone started clapping and cheering as we entered the ballroom at the Waldorf Astoria. We had the most perfect ceremony and now we'd have the perfect reception. The room was filled with over three hundred guests, including my parents and Lucas's father. Instead of going on a fancy honeymoon, we spent a week alone at the lake house. It was the first time we'd been away from Scarlett for more than a day.

"Do you think Scarlett is doing okay?" I asked Lucas as we laid in bed.

"She's doing just fine." He kissed me. "She's with your parents."

"Again, do you think she's doing okay?"

He let out a chuckle as his grip around me tightened.

"I'm sure she's giving your parents a run for their money. Do you have any idea how happy you make me?" The corners of his mouth curved upward.

"As happy as you make me?"

"More." He rolled me on my back and hovered over me. "I love you so much, Mrs. Thorne."

"And I love you so much, Mr. Thorne."

~

Six Weeks Later

*L*ucas

Raising a highly intelligent child was rewarding as well as exhausting. Scarlett demanded a lot of our attention and needed to be mentally stimulated at all times. At a year old, she was already saying more words than the average child.

I was sitting behind my desk when my office door opened, and Jenna walked in holding Scarlett.

"What a nice surprise." I grinned as I got up, kissed Jenna and took my daughter from her arms.

"Hi, princess." I tickled her.

"Daddy." She smiled.

"What are you doing here, babe?"

"I need you to watch her. The babysitter called and has the flu, my mom has an appointment of her own, and I have my doctor's appointment."

"I have a meeting in fifteen minutes."

"And? Do you want me to cancel my doctor's appointment and not get a refill on my birth control pills?"

"You know what, I'll just bring her to my meeting."

"Good idea." She smiled. "I love you. Just bring her home with you," she said as she hooked the diaper bag over my shoulder, gave me and Scarlett a kiss and walked out.

"Wait! You're not coming back to pick her up?"

"I have some errands to run. I love you!" She shouted as she walked down the hallway.

I looked at Scarlett who had successfully managed to untie my tie.

"Looks like you're spending the rest of the day with daddy." I kissed her head.

"Daddy." She smiled. "Juice."

I left the office a couple hours early because I wasn't getting any work done. Scarlett wanted nothing to do with any of my staff and she only wanted me. When I arrived home, I noticed Jenna wasn't back yet.

"Play with your blocks, princess," I said as I set Scarlett on the floor.

Pulling my phone from my pocket, I called Jenna.

"Hello."

"Hey, babe. I'm home with Scarlett. Are you on your way?"

"Yeah. I'll be home soon."

"Great. I miss you and I love you."

"I miss and love you too. See you soon."

"Book. Book," Scarlett said as she tugged on my pant leg while holding a book in her other hand.

Picking her up, I took her over to the couch and read to her. About thirty minutes later, I heard the elevator ding.

"Mommy's home, princess."

Walking over to the elevator, Jenna stepped out, gave me a kiss and took Scarlett.

"There's my genius girl. I missed you." She hugged her tight. "How did it go at the office?" She smirked.

"Why do you think I came home a couple hours early? She wanted nothing to do with any of the staff and she wouldn't let me put her down."

"So you cancelled your meeting?"

"Oh no. I took her in the conference room with me after I left her with Laurel, and she had a meltdown."

"Were you not being nice to Miss Laurel?" She tickled her. "So how was she in the meeting?"

"She was actually pretty good. I held her while I gave a power point presentation and she seemed fascinated with all the coding I had on there."

"My mom and dad will be here soon. They're going to take Scarlett for the night."

"Why?"

"I thought it would be nice for us to spend the evening alone."

"I love the way think, Mrs. Thorne." I kissed her lips. "I'm happy you worked things out with them. They sure have been a big help since they moved to New York a few months ago."

"I know and I'm grateful for that." She handed Scarlett back over to me. "I'm going to go pack her bag. Can you put her in her highchair and feed her?"

"Of course I can. Come on, princess. Let's get some food in your belly." I tickled her.

~

*J*enna

"How did you doctor's appointment go?" Lucas asked as he wrapped his arms around me from behind and kissed the side of my neck. "Did you get a refill on your pills?"

"Actually, that's what we need to talk about." I turned around in his arms.

"Talk about what?"

"I couldn't get a refill on my pills."

"Why not?" His eye narrowed at me.

"Because I'm pregnant, Lucas."

"You're what?"

"I'm pregnant. You know it's something that happens when two people have sex and one person screws up her pills, again."

"Ugh, Jenna. How could you let that happen again?"

"I know. But it's your fault."

"My fault? How is it my fault that you screwed up your pills again?"

"It just is, and when I think of the reason, I'll let you know."

He let out a chuckle and pulled me into him.

"We're having another baby."

"Are you happy about it?" I asked him as I broke our embrace.

"I'm very happy. How do you feel about it?"

"I walked around Central Park for over two hours asking myself

173

that. I mean, I'm happy that we created another child, but can we handle another one so soon with Scarlett? She's quite the handful."

"We can handle anything. What's one more kid to add to the mix? We have two hands. One for each of them. Plus, I think Scarlett will be happy to have a little brother or sister to play with. And with them being so close in age, they'll be best friends. Maybe this one will be a genius too, and they can have little Einstein conversations together." He grinned.

"Maybe."

"Come here." He pulled me into him again. "I love you and I love our growing family."

"I love you too. I'm going to get fat again and you're still going to have that sexy body and I'll hate you."

"Babe, your body is always sexy regardless if you're pregnant or not." He swooped me up in his arms. "Now, I'm going to take you to the bedroom and show you just how sexy you are." His lips pressed against mine.

CHAPTER 36

*J*enna

I stared at myself in the full-length mirror and couldn't believe my belly was already expanding for I was only eight weeks pregnant. My morning sickness was worse this time around and lasted longer into the day.

"Damn. Aren't you a sight for sore eyes," Lucas said as he walked into the room. "Are you admiring that sexy body of yours?"

"No. I'm looking at how I'm already starting to show and I'm only eight weeks."

"Don't women usually show earlier with the second pregnancy? I thought I read that somewhere."

I turned and looked at him.

"And where would you read that?"

"I don't know. Maybe in that baby book of yours."

"Maybe you're right." I sighed.

"Anyway, you can ask Dr. Lewis about it at your appointment today." He walked over and kissed me.

"Thank you for coming with me."

"Are you kidding? I wouldn't miss it for the world. I already missed the first half of your first pregnancy and I won't ever do that again.

Remember, you are my first priority, Mrs. Thorne." He went to kiss me, and I put my hand over my mouth and ran to the bathroom.

$\sim$

"I'm already starting to show, Dr. Lewis. Is that normal since I'm only eight weeks?" I asked her.

"Your body already has a head start from your first pregnancy and your uterus never truly goes back to the size it was before you were pregnant. So yeah, it's pretty common to start showing sooner."

"See. I told you." Lucas winked at me as he held my hand.

"Let's see if we can hear a heartbeat today, but I don't want you to worry if we can't."

I lifted up my shirt as she placed the doppler on my belly and moved it around. All I could hear was a bunch of static. I began to panic when I saw the look on her face.

"Is something wrong, Dr. Lewis?" I asked as I looked at Lucas.

"I would like to do an ultrasound."

"Why?" Lucas asked.

"I just need to check something. I'll be right back.

"Oh God, Lucas. Something is wrong," I spoke in a panic.

"Calm down, babe." He brought my hand up to his lips. But I could tell he was just as nervous.

A few moments later, Dr. Lewis walked in with an ultrasound machine. After squeezing the gel on my belly, she pressed the transducer down and began scanning my belly as Lucas and I intently watched on the monitor.

"Oh boy." She smiled. "Just as I thought."

"Thought what?" Lucas asked.

"See this right here? This is your baby. And see this one? This is also your baby."

"What?" I asked through gritted teeth.

"Congratulations, Mr. and Mrs. Thorne. You're having twins."

"No I'm not."

"Yes, you are, Jenna. This is Baby A, and this is Baby B."

"Oh shit," Lucas said as he laid his forehead down on my arm.

"I'll give you two some time to process this, and I want to see you back here in three weeks."

Lucas helped me up from the table, and I just sat there staring at the wall.

"Jenna, are you okay?"

"Do I look okay? We're having twins, Lucas. Not one, but two babies at the same time! Two! We can barely handle Scarlett and now we're having two more!"

"Well, at least you can't blame this one on me."

"Oh my God. Did you just really say that?"

"What? It's the truth. Twins run on the mother's side."

"I didn't know you were such an expert on twins!"

"Calm down, babe. We have months to prepare for this. We've already been through it once and we'll get through it again." He gripped my shoulders.

We went over to my parents' house to pick up Scarlett and tell them news. I had no idea twins ran in my family and I hated my mother for not telling me. The moment she opened the door, I pushed past her.

"Why didn't you tell me twins run in our family?" I spat.

"Twins? You're having twins?" she asked in shock.

"Yes, mother. I'm having twins. Who in our family is a twin?"

"Jenna, I have no clue. In fact, I had no idea that twins ran in our family. I'll have to do some investigating, and I'll let you know."

It turned out that my mother's great grandmother was pregnant with twins and when they were born, she gave them up for adoption because they were born out of wedlock. The family was so ashamed, they kept it a secret. The only way my mother found out was because she did some digging into the family history and stumbled upon the twin's birth certificates.

Three Months Later

*L*ucas

Jenna was now five months pregnant, and I knew we would soon be outgrowing the penthouse.

"Scarlett is finally asleep," I said as I walked into the bedroom and took off my shirt.

"I hate you. I hope you know that," Jenna said as she stared at my body.

"You love this body and what it does for you." I smirked as I crawled on the bed next to her. "In all seriousness, we need to have a discussion."

"About how much I hate you and your sexy body?" A small smile framed her face.

I grabbed her chin, pinched her lips together and gave her a big kiss.

"No. About the penthouse."

"What about it?"

"We're outgrowing it and I think it's time we moved. It's only a three bedroom and what if we have another baby?"

"Excellent point, Mr. Thorne." She reached over on her nightstand and handed me a piece of paper.

"What's this?"

"Your appointment with Dr. Sherman."

"What appointment? And who's Dr. Sherman?"

"He's the doctor who will be performing your vasectomy."

"Excuse me?" I arched my brow at her. "There's no way I'm—"

"Yes, you are."

"So let me get this straight. Because you can't remember to take your birth control on time, you want me to make sure we don't get pregnant again?"

"Yep." She nodded her head.

"Don't you think we should have discussed this first?"

"Nope. If you want to keep having sex, you'll get it done."

"I have four more months to fuck you freely, Mrs. Thorne."

"But wouldn't you rather get it done now so after the babies are born, we don't have to worry about it? You're going to have to heal and stuff."

I let out a sigh because she did have a point.

"Do you really want another baby after we have the twins?" she asked. "I mean, we'll have three children. That's kind of one more than I planned on having."

"True. Three kids are going to be a lot. Especially if these two are geniuses like Scarlett. Okay. I'll go and get it done. You've pleaded your case." I leaned over and brushed my lips against hers. "Now, back to the penthouse. I think we really need to move."

"A bigger penthouse?" she asked.

"I was thinking more of a townhome."

A wide smile crossed her face. "I love that idea."

"I knew you would. I'll call the realtor first thing tomorrow morning. In the meantime, I'm going to take as much advantage of you as I can before my procedure. Will that be a problem for you?"

"Not at all. But first stand up and take down your pants. Let me show you how much I hate you and your sexy body."

"Damn, Jenna," I said as I quickly unbuttoned my pants and stood up.

~

We brought Scarlett with us to the ultrasound appointment so see could see the babies. We were preparing her the best way we could for her sibling's arrival.

"Are we finding out the sex of the babies?" Dr. Lewis asked.

"Yes. Definitely." Jenna smiled.

"Babies," Scarlett said to Dr. Lewis.

"That's right, Scarlett. You're going to see your brothers or sisters."

Dr. Lewis squirted some gel on Jenna and pressed the transducer down on her belly. Tears sprung to my eyes when I saw my two precious babies snuggled together.

"They're so incredible," I said.

"Babies." Scarlett pointed to the monitor.

"That's right, princess. Those are your brothers or sisters in mommy's belly."

"The babies are doing excellent, Jenna. Let's see if I can tell what sex Baby A is. Baby A is a girl." She smiled at us.

Please let baby B be a boy. Please. Please. Please. I silently thought.

"And Baby B is—no doubt about this one. It's a boy."

"YES!" I shouted as I leaned over and kissed Jenna.

"Both babies are healthy and growing on schedule. I'm going to do a few more ultrasounds over the next few months to keep an eye on their positions. There may be a possibility we'll need to do a c-section, and I just want you to be prepared."

I helped Jenna from the table, and we stopped to get some lunch before our appointment to look at a couple townhomes. I was ecstatic we were having another girl, but secretly I was happier we were having a boy.

CHAPTER 37

*J*enna

The moment I stepped inside the home located at 12 East 80th Street, I felt something. An overwhelming feeling that this was the home we were meant to live in. I got that feeling just by standing in the foyer. I hadn't even seen the rest of the house, but somehow, I just knew.

"This is the one, Lucas," I said.

"Babe, we haven't even seen the rest of it yet."

"I know. But I can't explain it. This is where we are meant to raise our children."

"Well, let's take a look around first." He kissed the side of my head.

"How many bedrooms does this home have?" I asked the realtor.

"Eight bedrooms and ten bathrooms. So, after you have that baby, you'll have plenty room for more children."

"We aren't having any more children," I said. "I'm pregnant with twins."

"Oh my. Congratulations to you both. Well, then, you'll have plenty of rooms for house guests."

I fell in love with the entire house. From the gray colored walls, the beautiful oak flooring and the newly remodeled kitchen with custom white cabinets, Italian marble countertops and a stunning backsplash.

"The home hasn't been lived in for over two years. The couple that lived here passed away a couple years ago and their children had the place completely remodeled. It is turnkey ready as you can see. All you have to do is move your furniture in."

"May I ask how the previous owners passed away?"

"Jenna," Lucas whispered.

"What? That's important. I don't want to be living here if they died in this house."

"Unfortunately, they were killed in a boating accident in the Caribbean. They were on vacation and a storm hit while they were sailing."

"Oh no. That's so sad," I said.

"Yes. It was a tragedy. They raised their three children in this home and still lived here even when the children grew up and moved away. It's an excellent area and they were very happy here."

"And it's very close to my office."

"We'll take it," I said. "We'd like to make an offer."

"Excellent. Mr. Thorne, your thoughts?"

"You heard my wife. Let's make an offer and make this place our new home."

"I have one quick question. Why is the piano still here?" I asked.

"The sellers are leaving it as an option. If you don't want it, they will remove it."

"No. I want it," I said.

"What? Why?" Lucas asked.

"Because I play the piano and I think our children might like it too."

"And why have I never known this about you?" His brow raised.

"I don't know. I guess I never thought about it. If you had a piano when we first met, you would have known." I smirked.

"I guess the piano is staying," he said to the realtor.

"*A*re you okay?" I asked Lucas as I hooked my arm around him when he walked out of the room at the doctor's office.

"Just dandy, babe. Just dandy."

"You'll be fine as long as you follow the doctor's instructions."

"I just want to get home and lay down."

"Don't worry. You'll have plenty of time to rest. My parents are taking Scarlett for a couple days."

"Sounds good. I just want you to know I hate you." He took in a sharp breathe.

"Aw. That makes me feel so much better now that we hate each other." I reached up and kissed his cheek.

He shot me a look and I let out a snicker.

The moment we got home, he reclined back in the recliner in the living room while I went and grabbed an ice pack from the freezer.

"Here's your ice pack. I also brought you some Motrin."

"It hurts really bad, Jenna."

"Yeah. Well. Until you've experienced labor pains and pushed a 7lb 10 oz human out of your hole, I really can't sympathize with you. Not to mention the fact that I may be pushing out two humans from my vagina or having my stomach cut open to deliver them."

"Fine. You win."

I gave him a smile and kissed his lips.

"Take your Motrin like a good boy, and I'll make you a sandwich."

~

One Month Later

*L*ucas

I had made a full recovery and I was back in action. I really had no right to complain after what Jenna went through and will be going through with the twins, but damn did it hurt. Yesterday was moving day and we couldn't wait to be fully settled in our new home. We had hired Jimmy and Wes to repaint Scarlett's room and the twin's room. We kept Scarlett's room the same color as in the penthouse, and we painted the twin's room a light gray with all white furniture. One crib was decorated in pink bedding and the other was decorated with blue. We wanted to make sure we were prepared early just in case.

Scarlett was up the entire night, even when we brought her to bed with us, she wouldn't sleep. Jenna said it was because her mind was too stimulated from the move. Like I said, I loved having a daughter who was a genius, but it sure as hell was utterly exhausting at times. She wouldn't let us put her down and she wanted nothing to do with her toys.

Jenna was upstairs trying to organize things while I walked around the house with Scarlett as she continued to cry.

"Maybe this was a bad idea. The penthouse hasn't sold yet. Let's just move back there," I said.

Jenna thought that was hysterical and she couldn't stop laughing.

"What is wrong with you? She'll get used to it. Here, let me take her."

She took Scarlett over to the piano and set her on her lap. Jenna started to play a classical piece and immediately, Scarlett stopped crying.

"You are amazing," I said as I sat down on the bench next to her.

"Thanks. My parents forced me to start playing when I turned two. But I didn't mind. I liked it."

"Scarlett seems to like it too."

"I have an idea. Go get her booster seat. It's in the closet off the kitchen."

I got up, went to the closet, grabbed her seat and set it next to Jenna. She set Scarlett in the seat, buckled her in and got up from the bench, pushing it closer so Scarlett could reach the keys. She started hitting them with her tiny hands and laughed.

"Phew." I let out a sigh as I hooked my arm around Jenna and placed my hand on her large belly. "The babies seem very active today." I smiled at her.

"Tell me about it. They've been kicking all morning.

~

Six Weeks Later

*J*enna

"Well, Jenna. I'm sorry to say that Baby A has turned herself back around the wrong way. You're going to need a c-section."

"I guess she's a stubborn little girl like her mother." Lucas smirked and I smacked his chest.

"It happens all the time. I'm going to schedule your c-section for next Thursday since you'll be thirty-seven weeks. So whatever preparations you need to make, make them now. Of course, if you happen to go into labor before then, we'll take the babies then."

"Next Thursday is Lucas's birthday, so I think they can wait." I smiled at Lucas.

As the week went by, I started to get scared. Come tomorrow, I would have twin babies. As I lay in bed, Lucas wrapped his arm around me and softly stroked my belly.

"Soon we'll become a family of five," he said as he softly kissed my shoulder.

"I know. Who would have thought when we first met, we'd end up like this?"

"I'm happy you spilled your drink on me at the club," he said.

"And I'm happy you called me." I turned on my back.

"You know what really makes me happy?" he asked as he stroked my cheek.

"What?"

"That the condom broke, and you screwed up your pills." The corners of his mouth curved upward.

"I'm scared, Lucas. I'm really scared."

"Scared of what, babe?"

"That I won't be able to do it and fail my children."

"I think every parent feels that way. You are an amazing person and an amazing mother to Scarlett, and you will be just as amazing to

185

Serena and Samuel. I love you more and more every day, and I will be by your side forever."

Bringing my hand up to his face, I softly stroked it as I stared into his eyes. His lips were mere inches from mine until…

"Holy shit!" I placed my hands on my belly.

"What's wrong?"

"I think I'm in labor."

"Shit." I'll get dressed and grab your bag.

The pain was unreal and worse than what I had with Scarlett. I climbed out of bed and instantly fell to the floor. Lucas came running over and grabbed my arm.

"Babe, are you okay?"

"I was so looking forward to not experiencing this again."

"I know, babe." He helped me up.

"I already called a cab, and it'll be here in five minutes."

"What about Thaddeus?"

"He won't get here in time."

We took the elevator downstairs, so I didn't have to walk down, and when we stepped out the front door, the cab was waiting for us at the curb. I climbed in the back just as a contraction hit and let out a scream.

"Where to?" the cab driver asked.

"WHERE DO YOU THINK!" I shouted at him.

"Mount Sinai, please. And if you can really step on it, there will be a very big tip for you."

"Got it," he said as he pulled away from the curb and took off.

The guy was a total maniac and for a second I forgot about my contractions because I was too busy thinking about how I was going to die, pregnant with twins, in the back of a cab.

"Fast enough for you?" The cab driver asked with a smile as he pulled up to the emergency room.

"Yes. Thank you," Lucas said as he handed him some cash.

I could tell he was stressed out. The moment we entered the ER, I had to stop because I was in so much pain. Immediately, I was taken up to the Labor & Delivery Unit. I was put in a room and Lucas helped me change out of my clothes and into a gown. A nurse named Ella walked in and hooked me up to the fetal monitor.

"Dr. Lewis is on her way in now." She smiled. "Just try to relax."

"I would if I wasn't in so much pain."

As I was going through my contractions, Lucas was just standing there holding my hand.

"Why aren't you talking? Why aren't you telling me to breathe?!" I yelled at him.

"Because last time you threatened the shit out of me. I think it's best if I don't say anything."

"Oh my God. You're such an asshole sometimes."

"I know you don't mean it, babe. It's the pain talking."

Just as I was ready to yell some obscenities at him, a group of people walked in the room. A group of ten to be exact. The first five people introduced themselves and told me they were the team for Baby A, and the other five were for Baby B.

"Hello, Thorne family." Dr. Lewis smiled. "You just couldn't wait a few more hours, eh?"

"The babies want out. Like little prisoners who want out of jail."

Dr. Lewis laughed as she placed her hand on mine. She looked at the fetal monitor and then at her watch.

"How important is it that your babies are born on your husband's birthday?" she asked me.

"Very important."

"No, Jenna. It doesn't matter. I hate seeing you in so much pain. Just get the babies out now, Dr. Lewis."

"NO!" I shouted. "These babies are going to be born on your birthday.

"We have one hour until midnight. By the time I get you prepped, and we get the epidural in you, it'll be close. As long as the twin's heart rates don't take a dip and they don't show any signs of distress, I can wait to cut you open at midnight. Sound like a plan?"

"Yes." I nodded my head.

"Alright, folks, let's get Mrs. Thorne into the O.R. and prepped for surgery. Lucas, you'll need to change into a gown and wait here while we prep her. One of the nurses will come get you when we're ready."

"Okay."

Lucas leaned over and kissed my lips.

"I'll be by your side in a flash. I love you so much."

"I love you too. I'm sorry I called you an asshole."

"Don't be sorry. It's the truth." He gave me a wink.

When they wheeled me into the operating room, my eyes focused on the massive bright lights and the line of tools that were laid out. My heart started racing and I needed my husband. They transferred me from the bed onto the operating table. The anesthesiologist walked in, introduced himself and asked the nurses to help me sit up so he could administer the epidural. Once that was done and I was pretty much prepped, Lucas walked in and sat on the stool next to me. He grabbed my hand and brought it up to his lips.

"I'm so sorry for being such a baby after I had my vasectomy," he whispered.

"It's okay, babe. I still love you."

I could see the smile beneath his mask. Dr. Lewis walked in and looked at the clock.

"We have five minutes until midnight, Jenna. How are you doing?"

"I'm pain free at the moment, Dr. Lewis. So, I'm doing great."

"Excellent." She looked at the clock again. "Okay. The clock has struck midnight. Happy birthday, Mr. Thorne."

"Thank you, Dr. Lewis."

"Happy birthday, babe," I said to him.

"Thank you, babe. I'm so proud of you." He ran his finger across my head to distract me. "I can't wait to meet our daughter and son."

"Me either. But honestly, I can't wait to get them out of my body. I'm so over this pregnancy."

He let out a light laugh, and we heard Dr. Lewis.

"Your daughter is coming out. Here she is." Dr. Lewis held her up as she let out a scream.

Tears filled my eyes as I stared at her before she was handed off to one of the nurses.

"She's beautiful, Jenna," Lucas kissed my forehead as his eyes filled with tears.

"And here's your son," Dr. Lewis smiled as she held up our screaming little boy and then handed him off to another nurse.

Suddenly, they raced Samuel out of the room, and a nurse walked over to me.

"Jenna, your son is having a little trouble breathing so we're going to take him to the NICU for a bit."

I grabbed my husband's arm and looked at him as tears filled my eyes.

"Go. Go be with our son."

He ran out of the room as the tears streamed down my face.

Once the doctor finished closing me up, one of the nurses put Serena in my arms.

"Hi there. I've waited so long to meet you, beautiful girl. I'm your mom."

She was so beautiful and tiny. My heart ached for my son and all I wanted to do was hold him and tell him everything was going to be okay. The pain in my heart was unbearable. I wanted my son and my husband.

I was wheeled to my room and the nurse who was assigned to me brought me a bottle for Serena. I'd decided not to breastfeed the twins since my milk supply wasn't great to begin with and I had to stop with Scarlett within four months. I was consumed with fear for my son, and I couldn't think about anything else. Suddenly, Lucas walked into the room and ran over to me.

"He's fine, Jenna. Samuel is perfectly fine. The nurse said she'll bring him to the room in a few minutes."

"Thank God." I felt as if I could breathe again.

"Hey there, sweetheart." Lucas smiled as he touched Serena's cheek.

"Do you want to hold her and finish feeding her?"

"I would love to."

As soon as I handed her over to him, the nurse brought me my son. The moment she put him in my arms, I started to sob.

"Here's his bottle." The nurse smiled at me as she patted my arm.

"He looks just like you," I said to Lucas.

"You think so?" He grinned.

"He has your lips and nose. And your forehead. I can already foresee him being a little heartbreaker."

The corners of his mouth curved upward as he stared at me.

"What?" I smiled.

"Thank you."

"For?"

"For giving me the best birthday gifts of my life."

The next morning, my parents brought Scarlett up to meet her brother and sister. I wouldn't lie and say that Lucas and I weren't a little worried. Her entire world was changing, and we weren't sure how she was going to handle it.

CHAPTER 38

SIX WEEKS LATER

*L*ucas

I couldn't believe the twins were already six weeks old. This time around Jenna agreed to hiring some help. We hired a full-time housekeeper named Maria. She was an older Italian woman who made the best lasagna I'd ever had, and she could clean like nobody's business. Jenna and I really liked her, and she was quickly becoming a part of our family. But the most important thing was that Scarlett loved her too. Then there was Gemma. The nanny we hired to help with the twins.

I was sitting in my office when my phone dinged with a text message from Jenna.

"Hello, my lover. Looking for a little fun? Meet me at the Mandarin, Suite 3610. I'll be waiting."

With a smile on my face, I instantly replied.

"I'm on my way."

Grabbing my suit coat, I opened my office door and stepped out.

"Laurel, I'm heading to lunch. I'll be gone at least a couple of hours."

"Enjoy your lunch, Mr. Thorne."

"I intend to." I gave her a wink.

Thaddeus dropped me off at the Mandarin and I took the elevator up to the thirty-sixth floor. Knocking on the door of Suite 3610, Jenna opened it, grabbed my shirt and pulled me inside.

"You didn't tell me your doctor's appointment was today," I said as our lips tangled.

"I wanted to surprise you."

"Are you sure you're ready?" I asked as we made our way over to the bed.

"I've never been so ready for anything in my life."

She slid my suit coat off my shoulders and frantically unbuttoned my shirt as my hand untied her robe and it dropped to the floor.

~

"Are you okay?" I asked as I softly stroked her shoulder.

"I'm fine. Are you okay?" She lifted her head, and a beautiful smile crossed her lips.

"I've never been better. Do you hear that?"

"Hear what?"

"Exactly. It's quiet. No screaming Scarlett, no crying twins. Just pure silence."

"It's nice." She smiled as she brushed her lips against mine and then stared into my eyes.

"It is. Isn't it?" I brought my hand up and softly stroked her cheek. "Booking this suite was an excellent idea. I think we should do this at least twice a week. Rent a suite and escape for a couple hours. Just us. No children allowed." I smirked.

"I love that idea."

"Consider it done." I rolled her on her back and hovered over her. "I love you, Mrs. Thorne."

"I love you, Mr. Thorne."

~

*I*t was hard to believe the twins were going to be a year old in a week. Like their sister, they were highly intelligent children and we made sure their little brains were stimulated at all times. It was tough and exhausting, but we wouldn't trade it for the world.

When I walked through the door after a long day at the office, I could hear the screams of all three children. Scarlett was having a meltdown and the twins were sitting on the floor crying.

"What is going on?" I asked as I set my briefcase down.

"Scarlett wanted the toy Serena was playing with, so she took it from her. Serena started crying. When Sam heard her cry, he started crying. I took the toy away from Scarlett and told her it wasn't nice that she took it away from her sister, so she's having a meltdown."

I let out a sigh as I brushed my lips against Jenna's.

"I'll take Scarlett upstairs and calm her down while you calm down the twins, and hopefully peace in this house will soon be restored."

Jenna let out a laugh. "In about eighteen years or so."

~

*J*enna

I ended up coming down with the flu the day after the twin's first birthday party. At first, I thought it was food poisoning, but everyone else was fine. My life had been incredibly busy over the last couple of months between the kids, planning the twin's first birthday party and putting together a surprise party for Lucas. I was nauseous and extremely fatigued.

"Jenna, you've been feeling like this for a week," Maria said as she made me some chicken soup. "Is there a possibility you could be pregnant again?"

I let out a laugh. "God no. Lucas had a vasectomy when I was pregnant with the twins. We made sure we weren't having any more children."

"Sometimes they fail. I had a cousin who got pregnant five years after her husband had one."

"Was she sure it was her husband's?" I smirked.

"Well, it did cause some family drama at first, and he truly believed his wife had cheated on him. After the baby was born, a paternity test was done, and he was the father."

I swallow hard, as I set down my spoon.

"But if you had your period last month, all is good. I'm sure it's some nasty virus and it'll be gone soon."

I had been so busy last month I couldn't remember if I had a period or not. I hadn't even been keeping track since Lucas had the vasectomy.

"Jenna, are you okay?" Maria asked.

"I don't know, Maria. Thanks for the soup. I'm going to lay down for a while."

As I lay there, I thought about how there was no way I could be pregnant again. No possible way. There was only one way to find out. I ran to the store and picked up a test. It was so silly that I was even doing this. I had a virus. Or maybe something else was going on. Pregnant? No. Impossible.

I went into the bathroom, peed on the stick and waited. I laughed at myself for even thinking it. Once the test showed I wasn't pregnant, I'd call my general doctor and get in for a checkup and some tests. The timer on my phone went off so I picked up the stick and stared at the two pink lines staring back at me. My heart started racing, and I felt like I was going to pass out. Splashing some cold water on my face, I leaned over the counter and stared at myself in the mirror. How the hell was I going to tell my husband who had a vasectomy that I was pregnant again?

～

"We need to talk," I said as I grabbed his hand the minute he walked through the door and led him upstairs.

"Okay. Can I put my briefcase down first?"

194

"No!"

"Jenna, what is going on?" He asked as I closed the bedroom door.

"I have a question for you, Lucas."

"Okay?"

"After your vasectomy, did you ever get your semen checked? Remember you had the appointment scheduled for eight weeks later?"

"Um. You know. I believe I had to reschedule that appointment due to an emergency meeting. And I may have forgot. Why?"

"Why?" I cocked my head at him. "I'll tell you why."

I stormed into the bathroom, grabbed the stick and threw it at him.

"What the fuck, babe?" He furrowed his brows at me. "What is this?"

"What does it look like?"

He stared at the stick for a moment, and I could see the color drain from his face.

"I don't have the flu, Lucas. I'm fucking pregnant!" I shouted.

"No. No way. I had the vasectomy. This test is defective. It has to be. Did you try another one?"

"No."

"Well, didn't you have your period last month?"

"I don't remember!" I shouted.

"How can you not remember?"

"Because I was busy taking care of your three children and planning parties!"

He walked over to me and firmly gripped my shoulders.

"We both need to calm down. I'll run out right now and buy another test. Okay? The store is right on the corner."

"Okay." I nodded my head.

Within in fifteen minutes, he walked back into the room with a plastic bag and dumped five additional tests on the bed.

"Go on. Take them and let's find out for sure."

"I can't pee on command, Lucas."

"Then you need to start drinking because I'm freaking out here, Jenna."

"You're freaking out?" I shouted.

After drinking an entire bottle of water, I was able to take all five tests. As they were lined up in a row on the sink, we both stood there and watched as all five came up positive.

"You call your doctor in the morning, and I'll call mine," he said.

"This time it's your fault, and I want to hear you say it. Say it, Lucas!"

"It's my fault," he shouted. "There, are you happy now?" He walked out of the bathroom, sat on the edge of the bed and placed his face in his hands.

Sitting next to him, I placed my hand on his thigh.

"I'm sorry. I just can't believe this."

"I can't either."

He placed his hand on mine and brought it up to his lips.

"I guess it's meant to be that we're the parents of four children," he said.

"Or five."

"Don't say that, Jenna. Fuck."

"What are we going to do?" I asked.

"I don't know. Live life and raise our kids the best way we know how. Millions of couples have four or more kids. If they can do it, so can we. And one day, our kids will be all grown up, they'll move out, and we'll be sitting here wishing we had this time back."

"Somehow I don't think so," I shook my head.

"Yeah. Me either."

CHAPTER 39

*J*enna

At my eight-week checkup, I told Doctor Lewis I wanted an ultrasound because I couldn't wait to find out if we were having one baby or two. The anxiety was not only killing me, but Lucas as well.

"Okay. Are you ready?" Dr. Lewis asked.

Lucas grabbed my hand and held it tight as we stared at the monitor.

"There's the baby's heartbeat. It's nice and strong."

"There's only one heartbeat, right?" Lucas asked.

"Yes. There's only one baby in Jenna's belly."

"Are you sure?" he asked. "There isn't another one hiding anywhere?"

"Mr. Thorne, I promise you there's only one baby here." She smirked.

We both let out a sigh of relief.

"I don't mean to pry, but how did this happen? Didn't you have a vasectomy?" Dr. Lewis asked him.

"Apparently, the tubes reconnected," I said. "And he didn't bother to get his semen checked after the procedure."

"Okay. That explains it. Since you already had a c-section for the twins, we can do a c-section for this baby and I can tie your tubes if you want. I can promise you there will be no more babies in your future." She smiled.

"Thank you, Dr. Lewis. I was going to talk to you about that."

～

Eight Months Later

*L*ucas

At thirty-eight weeks, our son, Sebastian Lucas Thorne was born and weighed in at exactly eight pounds. I never thought in a million years I'd be back in this hospital holding my fourth child.

"He's beautiful." I smiled as I leaned over and kissed Jenna.

"He certainly is. I love you, Lucas."

"I love you too, babe." My lips brushed against hers.

～

Nine Months Later

*B*efore I even approached the door to the house, I could hear the screaming and crying. I stood there for a moment holding my briefcase and took in a long deep breath before stepping inside.

"What's going on in here?" I shouted over all the noise.

"Baby drama!" Jenna shouted back. "Welcome home, babe. Grab a kid or two and help me out here."

The corners of my mouth curved upward as I brushed my lips against hers. This was my life and my family, and as chaotic as it was at times, I wouldn't trade it for anything.

EPILOGUE

I wrapped my arms around Jenna as she stood at the kitchen sink and pressed my lips against her bare shoulder.

"Good morning." She smiled as she turned around in my arms.

"Good morning. I don't like waking up and you're not in bed." I brushed my lips against hers.

"I wanted to get the muffins in the oven before you woke up."

"Banana nut?"

"Of course." She grinned.

"Then you're forgiven. Listen, do you hear that?"

"Hear what? I don't hear anything."

"Exactly. Blissful silence. We need to enjoy it before the kids come up. What time will they be here?"

"Soon, I think."

"Is Scarlett bringing Alan?"

"I think so. I'm not sure though."

"I feel like I need to have a talk with that boy."

"Leave him alone, Lucas. He's a good kid."

"But I think they're getting too serious. She is only twenty-one."

"They've been dating for a year. He's her first love."

"I'm just not sure he's the right guy for her. Something's off with him and I can't quite put my finger on it."

"*T*hat's her decision. Not ours. Now go sit down and I'll bring you a cup of coffee and a muffin."

The lake house was our special place. More special than I originally thought it would be. The kids loved it here and were joining us for part of the summer. Scarlett was now twenty-one and working for the government in a lab in New York as a Molecular Biologist. Serena and Sam were nineteen and both were on track to graduate from Harvard in December before starting medical school in January to become neurosurgeons. As for Sebastian, our youngest child who was now seventeen, just completed his first year of college at Columbia. Out of all four children, he was the one who took after me and would be the one to take over Thorne Tech when I retired.

As Jenna and I were sitting at the table enjoying our coffee and muffin, the door opened, and Scarlett and Sebastian walked in.

"Hey, princess. Hello, son." I smiled when I saw them.

"Hi, Dad." Scarlett kissed my cheek. "Hi, Mom." She walked over and kissed Jenna.

"Hey, Dad." He fist bumped me. "Hey, Mom." He kissed her cheek. "Are those banana nut muffins?"

"They sure are. I made them just for you." Jenna looked at me and gave me a wink.

"You are the best mom ever! Hey, Dad, can we go fishing?"

"Of course. I already planned on it."

"Awesome. I'm going to go take a shower first. I got in a little late last night."

"Yeah, and I had to wake his sorry ass up this morning, or we would have missed our flight," Scarlett said.

"I would have woken up, you nerd," he said as he flew up the stairs.

Scarlett rolled her eyes as she grabbed a cup of coffee and sat down with us.

"So, is Alan coming up?"

"Um, no." She brought her cup up to her lips. "We broke up last week."

"Oh, sweetheart. I'm sorry." Jenna reached over and patted her arm.

"Please, Mom. I'm totally fine. I was the one that broke up with him."

"Why, princess?" I asked as I was smiling on the inside.

"He just wasn't—he wasn't—"

"Smart enough for you?" I asked.

"Lucas!" Jenna said.

"It's okay, Mom. Dad's right. He wasn't the one for me. I need someone who can hold intelligent conversations, and unfortunately, Alan, isn't that guy."

"You did the right thing, princess." I tried so hard to hold back my happiness and Jenna knew it as she narrowed her eye at me.

"Anyway, I figured I better tell you this now. I'm moving out. I found this great apartment in SoHo."

"I didn't know you were looking," I said.

"Daddy, I'm twenty-one and I'm a molecular biologist with an amazing job, making amazing money. It's time I move out and be on my own."

"This hurts, Scarlett. It really hurts."

"I know, Daddy, but you'll be okay." She smiled as she got up and kissed my cheek. "I'm going to go change."

I sat across from Jenna who wouldn't even look at me.

"How long have you known?" I asked.

"She told me last week over the phone and she wanted to be the one to tell you herself."

I let out a long sigh. "I guess our baby is finally growing up."

Jenna got up, took a seat on my lap and wrapped her arms around me.

"It's time to let her go, Lucas. Besides, we still have three other kids at home, when they're not away at college. Besides Sebastian, who commutes to Columbia."

"That's because he's a mama's boy." I arched my brow at her. "He isn't ever leaving."

"I secretly hope he doesn't." She kissed my lips.

As we were locked in a passionate kiss, the door opened, and the twins walked in.

"Ew. Stop that!" Serena and Sam both said at the same time.

❧

*A*s I stood at the grill, grilling the hamburgers and hot dogs, I stared at my boys as they sat in the boat and fished in the lake. Turning around, I smiled as I watched my daughters help Jenna set the patio table for dinner. This was my family, and they were all grown up. Time had flown by so quickly. One minute I was holding them in my arms, kissing their boo boo's, drying their tears, and the next minute, I was sending them off to college. Jenna and I never thought this day would come, but it had, and we were so proud of the family we raised. I never thought from the moment I laid eyes on her, this would become my life, and I thanked God every day for putting her in my path.

I took the burgers and hot dogs off the grill and set them in the center of the table.

"Looks good, Dad." Scarlett smiled as she kissed my cheek.

"Yeah, Dad. You're the best." Serena kissed my other cheek.

Walking down to the lake, I yelled to the boys that it was time for dinner. As they brought the boat back and climbed out, I hooked my arms around them.

"I love you, boys."

"We love you too, Dad," both Sam and Sebastian said at the same time.

"Are you okay?" Sam asked.

"I'm wonderful, Sam. Absolutely wonderful." I pulled both of them into me as we walked back to the house.

❧

J'd like to invite you to join my Sandi's Romance Readers Facebook Group where we talk about books, romance and more! Come join the fun!

You can also join my romance tribe by following me on social media and subscribing to my newsletter to keep up with my new releases, sales, cover reveals and more!

Newsletter
Website
Romancedwellshere
Facebook
Instagram
Bookbub
Goodreads

Looking for more romance reads about millionaires, second chances and sports? Check out my other romance novels and escape to another world and from the daily grind of life – one book at a time.

Series:

Forever Series

Forever Black (Forever, Book 1)
Forever You (Forever, Book 2)
Forever Us (Forever, Book 3)
Being Julia (Forever, Book 4)
Collin (Forever, Book 5)
A Forever Family (Forever, Book 6)
A Forever Christmas (Holiday short story)

Wyatt Brothers

Love, Lust & A Millionaire (Wyatt Brothers, Book 1)
Love, Lust & Liam (Wyatt Brothers, Book 2)

A Millionaire's Love

Lie Next To Me (A Millionaire's Love, Book 1)
When I Lie with You (A Millionaire's Love, Book 2)

Happened Series

Then You Happened (Happened Series, Book 1)
Then We Happened (Happened Series, Book 2)

Redemption Series

Carter Grayson (Redemption Series, Book 1)
Chase Calloway (Redemption Series, Book 2)
Jamieson Finn (Redemption Series, Book 3)
Damien Prescott (Redemption Series, Book 4)

Interview Series

The Interview: New York & Los Angeles Part 1
The Interview: New York & Los Angeles Part 2

Love Series:

Love In Between (Love Series, Book 1)
The Upside of Love (Love Series, Book 2)

Wolfe Brothers

Elijah Wolfe (Wolfe Brothers, Book 1)

Nathan Wolfe (Wolfe Brothers, Book 2)
Mason Wolfe (Wolfe Brothers, Book 3)

Standalone Books

The Billionaire's Christmas Baby
His Proposed Deal
The Secret He Holds
The Seduction of Alex Parker
Something About Lorelei
One Night In London
The Exception
Corporate A$$ETS
A Beautiful Sight
The Negotiation
Defense
Playing The Millionaire
#Delete
Behind His Lies
One Night In Paris
Perfectly You
The Escort
The Ring
The Donor
Rewind
Remembering You
When I'm With You
LOGAN (A Hockey Romance)
What If You